THE INCREDIBLE
SHRINKING DUNJER

I knew what was happening. My conscious-ness was intact and going great guns. It seemed to embrace all reality. I knew that, but the details were kind of fuzzy. I didn't worry about it. I didn't worry about anything.

Like a yo-yo, I felt myself beginning to reel in, to contract. I kept shrinking.

The galaxy pulled me toward it, drew me in from the far corners of the universe.

I was moving faster now, rushing along like the Happy City locomotive on full throttle.

Then the stars started to wink out.

And I was gone too...

*Don't Miss the First Exciting Adventure
in Happy City by*
Isidore Haiblum
from Avon Books

SPECTERWORLD

CRYSTAL WORLD

ISIDORE HAIBLUM

AVON BOOKS • NEW YORK

CRYSTALWORLD is an original publication of Avon Books. This work has never before appeared in book form. This work is a novel. Any similarity to actual persons or events is purely coincidental.

AVON BOOKS
A division of
The Hearst Corporation
1350 Avenue of the Americas
New York, New York 10019

Copyright © 1992 by Isidore Haiblum
Cover illustration by Gary Ruddell
Published by arrangement with the author
Library of Congress Catalog Card Number: 91-93003
ISBN: 0-380-75859-8

First AvoNova Printing: February 1992

AVONOVA TRADEMARK REG. U.S. PAT. OFF. AND IN OTHER COUNTRIES, MARCA REGISTRADA, HECHO EN U.S.A.

Printed in the U.S.A.

RA   10   9   8   7   6   5   4   3   2   1

CHAPTER 1

The mech intercom buzzed me. "Humperdink Sass to see you, boss," it said.

"Sass?"

"That's what he claims," the mech voice told me. "Frankly, the little person appears quite suspicious."

"What's he doing?"

"Muttering to himself."

"Probably trying to square the universe," I told the mech.

"Shall I have the guards beat him to a pulp?"

"No, just send him in; I like to save the fun part of this business for myself."

I sat back in my swivel chair, glanced out of my ninety-first floor window. Happy City stretched out below me; mostly it appeared to be intact. Copters still dotted the sky. Cars still buzzed along the multilevel drives. So probably I was safe. Only I didn't feel safe. The little crackpot was a certified scientific genius, and we were pals. He was also a menace. Every time we met up, something terrible happened, usually on a grand cosmic scale.

The office door opened.

The peculiar little person standing in the doorway had a round bald head with tufts of white hair behind each ear. A short Vandyke beard accented his cherubic features. His gray toga and sandals matched his eyes perfectly.

"Dunjer," Dr. Sass said, beaming, striding toward the visitors armchair.

"He just left," I told him. "If you rush to the speed lift maybe you can catch him."

"Ha!" he said, "I see the lack of a crime wave hasn't dented your spirits."

"Crime's doing fine, thanks. And so are my spirits which I imbibe directly from the bottle."

Security Plus, the private outfit I headed up, was the chief crime stopper in Happy City. It was composed of some human ops but mostly of mechs, which unlike the city constables, couldn't be bribed. Making them worth every penny we squeezed out of our customers.

Sass seated himself comfortably. "Your worries are over, Dunjer."

"I didn't know I had any."

"You are president of this corporation?"

"Yeah, the last time I looked."

"Then you have worries, if not for yourself, then for the shareholders in this firm, not to mention the personnel who are dependent on you for their livelihood."

"The mechs will appreciate your concern, Doc; sometimes they get very anxious about being rewired and lubricated on time. Our stockholders are still trying to get over the tax bite on the last crime wave. Actually, I'm enjoying the peace and quiet."

"The bonanza I am about to offer you will drive all thoughts of peace and quiet from your mind, Dunjer."

"That's what I was afraid of. Why can't you be a good sport and offer this bonanza to one of our competitors, eh?, some small outfit on the make; they won't mind and neither will I."

Sass scowled. "This unseemly tendency to jest in the face of grave occurrences does not do you credit, Dunjer."

"Grave yet. Now you've really got me scared. Just what is this surefire bonanza you've brought me?"

"A great opportunity. During my travels I encountered a government besieged by spies, informers, and saboteurs."

I shrugged. "What government isn't?"

"Ah, but the stakes are high here. There is a slight dispute with a neighbor that could quite possibly flare up, even get out of hand. The authorities, as you might well imagine, are distressed that their defense plans could fall into wrong hands."

"The authorities always worry about little things like that. These guys aren't the aggressors are they?"

"Perish the thought, Dunjer."

"Too bad. I charge double for aggressors."

"Then you are interested?"

"On behalf of Security Plus I'm always interested; it says so in my contract. And that little document was constructed by artists. It's just when you start messing around with the universe, Doc, that I get a bit edgy.''

"Have no fear, Dunjer; this is a simple open-and-shut matter.''

"Aren't they all?''

"Trust me.''

"Uh oh. This gets worse by the minute. What's the deal, Doc, I go ten rounds with their heavyweight champ? Or is it something easy, like a fight to the death in the local arena?''

"You certainly do carry on, Dunjer. The Magalonians are a peace-loving people. They wish merely to cultivate the arts and tend to their lands.'' Sass beamed at me. "Sounds idyllic, does it not?''

"Actually,'' I said, "it sounds rather dull.''

"Well, perhaps, but their next-door neighbors make up for it. The Ul are just the opposite—gross, hostile, and utterly unfeeling. In short, they are cads.''

"You saw them?''

"The Magalonians told me.''

"Uh huh.''

"There is no need to uh huh me, Dunjer; the Magalonians possess one overriding virtue that attests to their complete trustworthiness.''

"Universal lobotomies?''

"A huge treasury.''

I nodded thoughtfully. "Yeah, that might do it.''

"The initial dispute was over a parcel of land that both sides claimed. The Magalonians were triumphant in that one. But the Ul never forgave them.''

"Sore losers, eh?''

Sass wagged his head. "They lack class. Or so the Magalonians have assured me.''

"And why would they lie? What's the current hassle about?"

"The Ul want everything now."

"Everything of *what*?"

"Of Magalone, of course."

"Nothing like thinking big," I said. "As long as things stay verbal."

"Nothing but talk," Sass assured me.

"And these Magalonians figure they've got a case of the spies?"

"Director Trex is sure of it."

"Who's he, the president?"

"More like the dictator, Dunjer."

"I thought they were the good guys," I complained.

"They are," he said. "Emergency measures *had* to be taken in the face of the enemy. The dictator—er, director—was most reluctant to accept such awesome responsibility."

"Someone twist his arm?"

"Dear me, no. With martial law in effect that would be a capital offense." The little man gave me a loony smile. "Director Trex, you know, is the chief scientist of Magalone. He and I, you might say, are part of the great scientific community."

"I might. But don't count on it."

"On his shoulders rests the awesome duty of defending the motherland. He is chairman of the Defense Committee, and, of course, has free rein when it comes to expenditures. In fact, the entire treasury is at his disposal."

I nodded. "And what do you get out of all this, Sass? As if I didn't know."

"Why, a finder's fee. A mere pittance under ordinary

circumstances, but these are far from ordinary. Director Trex is prepared to go to any lengths to safeguard his country. I am sure that your end of the take, my dear Dunjer, will be quite spectacular. Quite.''

I settled back in my chair, regarded Sass sourly. ''And if my end isn't big enough, I suppose I could always knock over the treasury and make a run for it, eh, you little creep?''

His countenance was bland. ''Whatever you think best, Dunjer. I know I can rely on your judgment in these matters.''

''Yeah, but are you sure your pals are all that reliable? Do they really have enough dough to spend on a so-phisticated, up-to-the-minute state-of-the-art outfit like Security Plus?''

''Of course.''

''Well, I'm not so sure. I've never heard of this Ma-galone. Which means they're halfway across the globe somewhere, and probably on the lower end of the civi-lization scale. If we take 'em to the cleaners, all we're liable to get is a pair of used shorts and a worn shirt. I've had a go at a couple of the more backward city-states in this area; they talk big, but when it comes to the payoff it's usually in nickels and dimes.''

''But, Dunjer, Magalone is no puny city-state.''

''So what is it, some penny-ante fiefdom?''

''Magalone is a country.''

''What country? There aren't any.''

''Of course there are.''

''Then why haven't I heard of it?''

''Because it is in another dimension.''

CHAPTER 2

"It is really quite simple," I said. "Though actually, I don't understand any of it."

"Then how do you know it's simple?" Laura asked.

I squirmed in my chair. "Sass said so."

"Thomas," she said, "every time you've listened to that man, you've landed in the soup."

"Yeah," I admitted, "not to mention in a pickle and a jam."

"So?" Laura Fallsom had long blond hair, intense green eyes, and a buxom figure—just now wrapped in a blue and pink flower-print gossamer dress—which could drive men mad. To preserve sanity in the firm, I'd immediately made her my chief junior exec, put her to work directing mechs—who being already nutty were at least partially impervious to her charms—and began dating her myself; the boss, after all, should lead when it comes to taking risks. That she was a crackerjack op in all respects didn't hurt any either. I'd've planted a smooch on her round cheek just to keep in practice, but with XX41, one of our new chief double-X mechs, and O'Tool, a human op, looking on, I restrained myself.

I sat up in my chair. "This time," I told Laura, "the main dish isn't pickles and jam, it's kale, spinach, and cabbage—otherwise known as the green stuff—namely dough in its pure, pristine form. Naturally, it can become bread or just about anything else the heart desires. You dig?"

"I think I get the picture, kiddo," she said.

"Right. And there's too much of it floating around in this damn Magalone to turn down."

"*Where*?" O'Tool asked. He was a tall, narrow guy with a long reddish face, creased brow, and sparse black hair. He had on a gray, three-piece business suit and red tie.

"Yeah," I said. "That's the tricky part, all right. You've put your finger on it."

"I have? This'll be the first time in weeks I've done anything right. You sure?"

I got up, went to the coffee machine, filled three mugs, and carried them back to the round table. I resisted the urge to pour the steaming liquid over O'Tool's noodle, seated myself, and took a swig of java. We were in the Security Plus conference room. Outside, the mid-morning sun blitzed through the windows. I'd taken the old orb for granted up till now, something as permanent as mismanagement in Happy City City Hall or five o'clock shadow. I was going to miss it, even if this Magalone had two or three suns hanging around that were twice its size. Maybe great wealth would make up for my temporary loss.

"You remember Dr. Sass' activator?"

Three heads nodded in unison.

"Well, as you know, the activator lets you pop up in the alternate worlds. And, as if that weren't bad enough, in the specter worlds as well, which are offshoots of the alternate worlds and no place to be. The trouble with Sass, besides being pesky and a crackbrain, is that he doesn't leave well enough alone. His dumb activator has now got him into some other dimension, where the worlds are almost just like here, only our doubles aren't running the show. You'd think that alone would be an improvement, but they're in the same mess as everyone else. Sass talked us up big in a place called Magalone. The head guy there doesn't know whom to trust, but he figures we're probably safe since we come from another dimension. Little does he know, eh? He's willing to shell out big bucks in any form we want—gold, diamonds, marbles, worthless paper money, you name it—for our services. All we gotta do is sweep his labs free of spies. At least that's something we know how to do."

"In this other dimension, uh?" O'Tool demanded.

"That's where the money is," I admitted.

O'Tool held up a lean palm. "Count me out!"

"Frankly, skipper," XX41 said, "despite my legendary devotion to duty, I was kind of hoping I'd make it into retirement."

"And do what?"

"Become a household fixture?"

"You wouldn't like being a lamp stand," I told it. "Besides, it's perfectly safe. Sass has gone into this dimension dozens of times. And I wasn't asking you to go along, O'Tool. You and Miss Fallsom will stay here and run things while I'm away."

"Oh, no I won't," Laura said.

"Won't?" I said.

"Stay here. Every time something interesting, exciting, and *deadly* happens, you want me to stay here."

"Deadly?" XX41 said accusingly. "I thought it was perfectly safe."

"She said it, not me," I pointed out. "Besides, few things are really perfect."

"If it's so safe," Laura said, "why can't I come?"

"Because it might be *deadly*," I yelled.

"See?" XX41 said.

"I resign," Laura said.

"So do I," XX41 said.

"Okay, okay," I said. "Jeez. You can stay," I told XX41. "And you can go," I told Laura. "And I get to take two giant steps. Is everyone happy now?"

"You're really letting her go?" XX41 said.

"Sure."

"Then it must be safe."

"Didn't I say so?"

"I'll go too then," XX41 said.

"That's very kind of you," I said.

"As long as it's safe."

"I've always wanted to see another dimension," Laura said.

"This is your big chance, kid."

"Thanks, boss."

"Thank Dr. Sass. He's the one who made it possible."

"He's going too?" Laura asked.

"Only to drop us off. When it comes to spies, the doc's strictly an amateur."

* * *

"Yes, Dunjer," Dr. Sass said, "you will need a sizable contingent of mechs, a quantity of spotter eyes, catcher ears, wiretappers, and personnel homing devices if you wish to succeed in Magalone."

"And if I wanna fail?"

"Then you just go about business as usual."

"My, we are in a sour mood today," I said, "aren't we?"

"You fail to realize the seriousness of this venture."

"So tell me."

We were back in my office. It was mid-afternoon. I had spent the morning briefing the human ops and double-X mechs on their chores during my absence. I'd had a heart-to-heart chat with the master control board who assured me it'd carry on gamely while I was gone. The alarm board hoped I wouldn't miss its unfailing alarm in the face of danger on this trip. I had lunch with Laura who refused to change her mind about going along, despite my best efforts. Making me wonder if *I* ought to change *my* mind about going along and just send her. And now I was back in the ring with old Sass.

"I have researched the matter. Magalone, in its day," he said, "was a model democracy, a sterling example for other states to emulate. One that served as a world-wide beacon, you might say."

"When was its day?"

The little man pulled thoughtfully at his Vandyke. "Fifty years ago, give or take a day."

"How time flies."

The little man nodded. "Martial law was indeed a grim necessity. Otherwise *everything* would have been lost." Sass looked appropriately grim. "Including the treasury. As it is, Magalone is still a bastion of freedom on that blighted world. But if the dreaded Ul win, freedom will be set back a thousand years.''

"They call themselves 'the dreaded Ul'?"

"The Magalonians call them that."

"The Ul got a lot to live up to."

"Don't we all," Sass said piously.

"And where'd you get all that stuff about freedom being set back a thousand years?"

"Why, the Minister of Information, of course. He has prepared a very expensive full-color brochure on the topic."

I sighed. "Nothing personal, Doc," I said. "You're dead sure these guys can foot the bill?"

Sass brightened. "About that, as I have said, there can be no question. Director Trex not only has unlimited access to the treasury, but can override any objections from the People's Senate or Committee for National Survival."

"And probably any objections *we* might have about our fee, when the job's done."

Sass shook his head. "I doubt that very much. Director Trex would hardly seek hostilities on two fronts, as it were. It's all he can do to keep himself afloat as it is. And in any case, money means nothing to him, only what money can buy."

"In this case, *us*."

"To rid him of these spies."

I lowered my voice. "Just between us, there really are spies, or is the old boy paranoid?"

"He seems to think there are spies." Sass grinned. "And that is what really matters, isn't it, Dunjer?"

* * *

I stood in the Security Plus assembly hall, Laura and Dr. Sass at my side, and reviewed my forces. "Okay, men," I said, "this is it." Twenty-four mechs looked back at me. Somehow, "men" didn't seem quite the right word. "You've all got your gear—some of you, as a matter of fact, *are* gear—and you know what to do. No one's going to challenge you, since Trex's given us the high sign, and what he says goes.

"Now, we're moving into strange, uncharted territory. So if you spot anything that looks even remotely like hostile action aimed our way, give me a buzz, and I'll get us out of there in a jiffy. Or more properly speaking, Dr. Sass will. He's worked out an interdimensional alarm system that'll be attached to both his activator and our alarm board. At the first sign of trouble he'll yank us back to Happy City, none the worse for wear.

"Any questions?"

There weren't any.

I nodded at Sass. "Ready when you are."

We went.

CHAPTER **3**

The man peered at us, nodded glumly, and said one word: "Welcome." He sounded as though he wasn't quite sure what the word meant—something unpleasant maybe—but was willing to give it a try.

He was seated behind a long desk, a tall, wiry guy in his late fifties with high cheekbones, a dark mustache, long nose, bags under his hazel eyes, a lined forehead, and black eyebrows under a shock of white hair. He wore glasses, a tan lab coat over an open-necked red and yellow striped shirt, and a large watch around one bony wrist.

The dictator himself, no doubt.

Aside from the man and desk the room was completely empty, or had been until we showed up. Nothing like a bunch of mechs to make for lots of company—depending on how you defined that word.

Dr. Sass stepped forward, waved a hand as though he were trying to conduct an orchestra, and beamed the smile of a man who expects to collect a large finder's fee. "Director Trex, allow me to introduce Tom Dunjer, president of Security Plus, and his charming associate, Miss Laura Fallsom."

The director allowed it, though judging by his pained expression, it was against his better judgment.

He nodded.

Laura gave him a cheery hello, as befitted an exec who was about to become filthy rich. I smiled pleasantly, no doubt inspired by the same motive.

Sass went on. "And their tried and true Security Plus brigade, of course, the fearless mechs I told you about." He actually got an arm around XX41's shoulder, as though he and it were inseparable buddies.

"We also do housecleaning if there are no spies around," XX41 spoke up.

Trex frowned. "I should hope so considering what you cost."

"Worth every penny," the mech said, "at least for the housework."

"Never encourage it to talk," I told Sass. "It's even worse than you."

"I don't mind telling you," Trex said, giving me the eye, "I would never pay your exorbitant fee if this were not a dire emergency." He nodded toward Sass. "Your agent here drives a merciless bargain."

"Yeah," I said, "we send him traipsing around the universe so he can drum up business. In between he takes turns browbeating our clients."

"Pay no attention to them," Laura cooed. "Why don't

you tell me about your problem.''

"My problem? It is the country's problem. I merely bear the immense burden. Spies," Trex said darkly. "Saboteurs. Enemy agents. They will be the undoing of us all.''

"From those nasty Ul?" Laura said.

"Who else, my dear Miss Follsom, but the vile Ul would do such a thing?" He removed his glasses, peered around the half-darkened room as if trying to make sure no rotten Ul were lurking there. "They are our closest neighbors. The other countries are too far away to get in their licks. But the Ul make up for it.''

Sass said, "Has a familiar ring to it, doesn't it, Dunjer?''

"For this we had to go to another dimension?" I said.

"Don't you worry your head about the bad old spies," Laura said. "We can take care of them, Director Trex, that's our specialty. And you can go on to the important things you have to do.''

"That would be the war," Trex said.

"War?" I asked. "What war?''

"*The* war," Trex said. "If there wasn't a war going on, man, do you think we'd be so worried about spies?''

"No one told me about any war," I complained, turning to Sass.

"Well, there is one," Trex said. "And you'll have to earn every cent I pay you.''

"It depends entirely on how you define war," Sass said. "Do try and remember that.''

"I'll be too busy ducking bullets to remember anything.''

"Better than ducking lasers," Sass said.

The whole lot of us were trooping down a long hallway, following in the director's wake.

"War is war," I told Sass, "and war is hell. Personally, I prefer a nice vacation resort to Hell."

"Yes, yes," Sass said impatiently. "But no armed conflict has emerged. That is my point, Dunjer. So far, it is only a war of words."

"You're sure, eh?"

"Of course I am."

"I'd've brought my dictionary if I'd known."

"This," Trex said with a note of pride in his voice, "is the dome."

No doubt about it, it was a dome, all right. But when you knew that, just what did you know?

We had stopped on a balcony overlooking a courtyard. I craned my neck, glanced up. The dome was transparent and curved away in all directions. It was night out there.

"It's very nice," Laura said.

Trex wrinkled his brow. "Nice?" he said. "Nice?" He seemed outraged by the notion.

"She means awful," XX41 put in quickly. "Long trips confuse her sometimes so she doesn't know what she means."

"I beg your pardon?" the director said.

"I know *precisely* what I mean," Laura said.

"The trip took only a moment," Dr. Sass said. "No one could call that long."

"Let me handle the diplomatic end of this mission," I whispered to XX41.

"Just trying to help, skipper. Some days, a mechanical's wisdom and insight can save the day."

"This isn't one of those days," I told it. To Trex I

said, "What about the dome, Mr. Director?"

Trex wagged an eyebrow at me. "The proper form of address is Your Directorship. But you may simply call me Dr. Trex. The dome, Mr. Dunger, extends over the entire capital. It is a marvel of engineering, impervious to even the most powerful weapons. It is, naturally, my creation. And so far, it has stymied the Ul."

"Uh huh. I almost understand that," I said. "Except for one small point."

"And that is?"

"Why these Ul don't go and level the rest of your country."

Trex all but smirked. "They are afraid."

"A cowardly lot, I take it," Sass said.

"On the contrary," Trex said. "They are superb fighters."

"Then the Magalonians must be even better," Laura said.

The director pulled at his chin. "My fellow countrymen, I fear, are mediocre warriors at best." He drew himself up to his full height. "The mere thought of the weapons created in my shop," he said, "holds the Ul at bay. It is why I was chosen director. The contribution that I have made to the defense effort has preserved the peace. I take credit for that."

"Credit where credit is due," Sass said. "As one scientist to another."

"Of course," Trex said. "I must say *your* achievements, Dr. Sass, have impressed me no end."

"If you must say so, go right ahead," Sass told him.

The director held up a finger. "It is the sole reason I have employed your countrymen."

"City-state men, actually," I said.

"You won't be sorry, Your Directorship," Laura said.

"You may call me Harold, my dear," he said, smiling. To the rest of us he said, "My own intelligence force has been infiltrated and corrupted. The capital is full of people willing and eager to sell themselves to the dastardly Ul. Even my own staff is suspect, not to mention the scores of technicians, workers, and delivery men who pass through our gates every day. My research is at a critical juncture just now. Security must be maintained. The future of Magalone may rest in your hands, Mr. Dunjer."

"Their hands, actually," I said, nodding toward the mechs. "When it comes to the heavy stuff, we let the mechs handle it. They don't get back strain, muscle cramps, or hernias."

"And they can't be bribed," Sass said brightly, echoing the company motto.

"So you've said," Trex said darkly. As though our mere presence here had turned us into suspicious characters.

"Follow me," Trex said.

We followed.

CHAPTER 4

"How you doing, kid?" I asked Laura.

"A little more hiking and I go back for my combat boots."

We were tagging along after the director again, down another long, winding corridor. The grand tour was beginning to seem a bit too grand, not to mention endless.

"Yeah," I said, "there's nothing like being in the field to make you miss the office. Don't say I didn't warn you."

"You didn't warn me."

"Next time I'll put it in writing."

"Why are we traipsing around like this, Thomas?"

"Because out here Trex's the boss and he feels like it. Maybe he thinks the mechs need a workout."

We passed a couple of armed soldiers in gray-blue

uniforms standing guard, the first we'd encountered. Large double doors were up ahead. More guards were clustered around them.

Laura said, "Looks like we're coming to something important."

"Probably another dumb corridor. Next he'll have us walking in circles."

"Now, Dunjer," Sass piped up, "remember Director Trex is no ordinary director."

"Right, he's crazy."

"On the contrary, he is a man of genius, a great scientist. You must expect such men to be, er, somewhat eccentric."

"You ought to know, pal."

The guards saluted and Trex pushed through the double doors. The whole caboodle of us, mechs and all, followed suit.

We found ourselves in a huge circular domed hall.

"I have taken you here by a circuitous route," the director said, "to avoid detection. The hallways through which we have come are totally secure. It will enable you to begin operations before anyone is the wiser."

"See?" Sass said.

"Yeah," I said. "A plan of sheer genius."

"Here," Trex said, "we are safe."

I glanced around. Something that looked like a small mountain shared the space with us, rose some ten stories high to the very top of the transparent dome. Trex turned a sappy smile our way, nodded toward the mountain, as though he were showing off a prize poodle. "Beautiful, isn't it?"

"Damn inspiring," I said. "You use it for skiing or what?"

Sass dug an elbow into my ribs, said to our host, "His line of work, I am afraid, has turned him into something of a cynic."

"You've blown it again, kiddo," Laura whispered.

The director shrugged. "How could he possibly know? This way," he said, with a sweep of his arm like a head waiter showing the customers to their table.

We all managed to squeeze into a gigantic tubular, glass-enclosed lift and were carried up the side of the wall. "Nice view of the mountain," I told Trex.

"Isn't it though?" he said, beaming, as though the slab of rock were a brilliant offspring who had just won a grade-school spelling bee. "The laboratory was especially built around it."

"Uh huh," I said, wondering if maybe the director was missing a screw or two. I didn't worry. A mere screw or two would still put him way ahead of most of our clients.

We stepped out on the top floor. The mountaintop poked through a hole in the floor as if anxious to see what was going on up here. I was kind of curious myself.

There was plenty of hardware around. It ran up the walls and crowded the desks and workbenches. The mechs must have felt right at home seeing their blood brothers take up so much space. The setup vaguely reminded me of our Security Plus master computer back at headquarters. Old Flutter Brain, as some of the staff called him, was a deep thinker who could run circles around a bevy of ordinary mortals. But next to this thing, in size at least, it was still a toddler. Size and brainpower, however, aren't necessarily related.

"That a computer?" I asked.

The director nodded. "In part."

"What's the other part?"

"Our salvation." And he rubbed his hands together.

"Uh huh. I'm glad I asked," I said. "Otherwise, I might have remained befuddled and ignorant."

Trax held up a hand. "Have no fear, Mr. Dunjer. I have brought you here to explain. What you are all looking at is the Destabilizer."

"I'd never've guessed."

"I certainly hope not," Trex said. "It is top secret."

"And what exactly does it do?"

"Why, it destabilizes, of course."

I bobbed my head. "I'm sorry I asked."

"It is a weapon," Sass said, "of gigantic power."

"The ultimate weapon, Mr. Dunjer."

"Just Dunjer will do," I said.

"We have worked on it for years," Trex said. "Around the clock. Ceaseless, backbreaking effort."

"Pretty quiet now," I said.

"I have given the entire staff the night off."

"Bonus holiday?"

"They too are suspect." He gazed around at his handiwork. "Time and again, Dunjer, this project has been victimized by a series of mishaps that have all but derailed it."

"Inside job, eh?"

"What else can it be?"

I was going to say mismanagement, but thought better of it.

"If it were not for the Knowledge Crystal, we would surely have faced utter ruin."

"The whosis what?" I asked.

"Our helpmate," Trex said with obvious satisfaction.

"It is a crystal formation that is a natural data synthesizer and repository."

I nodded knowingly. "A kind of supercomputer."

The director's eyes seemed to glow. "Far greater than any computer ever devised. Thousands of times greater!"

"Sounds great, all right. Got it under lock and key, I hope."

Trex grinned. "That is hardly necessary."

I regarded him with some curiosity. "Not afraid one of your spies, saboteurs, or traitors will run off with it?"

"That would be impossible."

I looked at the mountain. "Don't tell me," I said.

Trex nodded. "Very good, Dunjer."

I stared at the hunk of rock. "How does it work?"

"We have cables that feed directly from it into the Destabilizer computer." He waved at the hardware climbing the walls. "That is our primary means of communication. We have others."

"Such as?"

"Clear your mind."

"Eh?"

"Make it a blank," he said.

"Should be easy for you," Laura said sweetly, taking my arm.

"You will find it is an amazing experience," Sass said.

"I'll clear my circuits," XX41 said.

"Yeah," I said. "You and the rock should have lots in common."

I closed my eyes and pretended I was far away from here; actually, it wasn't such a bad idea. I was at the seashore with the waves lapping at the beach. The sky was clear and blue. I lay down next to my sand castle and tried to look through a window to see if anything interesting was happening. It wasn't. Neither was the amazing experience Sass had promised. I got rid of the beach, tried to wipe my mind clean as if it were a blackboard slate. Our host, Laura, Sass, and XX41 dropped away. The mechs winked out. I was alone in the darkest of nights. I waited. From somewhere far off a tiny voice spoke in my head. $E = mc^2$, it said. "Eh?" I said. *Use one cup of oats to three cups of water,* the voice told me. "What?" I said. *Do not forget to stir,* the voice reminded me urgently. "Jeez," I said. *It is always true,* the voice said, *that if p implies q implies r then p implies r.* "Uh huh," I said. *That was no woman, that was my wife! Ha. Ha.* "Ha, yourself," I said. *Iron only on the coarse side,* the voice instructed. "What can you tell me about the Destabilizer?" I asked. *I am afraid that is classified information,* the voice said. I opened my eyes.

Trex was beaming at me. "Well?"

"That was a very silly conversation," I said.

The director nodded gravely. "The Knowledge Crystal does have its silly side."

"Don't we all?" Laura said.

"Anyone else tune in on that?" I asked.

"It gave me a lot of homemaking hints," Laura said. "I almost learned how to bake peach pie."

"Anything about cooking oats?"

"Uh uh," she said. "But it told me I shouldn't wash colored clothes with white."

"Different message," I said.

"The Crystal," Sass said, "suggested a few refinements for the activator. Quite intriguing."

"We discussed advanced robotics," XX41 said. "I

believe I was able to enlighten it on some specific points where it had gone astray.''

"You were, eh?'' I turned to Trex. ''And what's your take on all this?''

''I instructed the Crystal not to divulge classified information,'' he said.

"Don't worry, it didn't. At least it's not a blabbermouth; that'll make my job easier. But how come I was handed all that disjointed gobbledygook?''

''And why was I given those silly household tips?'' Laura asked.

Trex put his hands behind his back, looked thoughtful. ''It adjusts to the receiver's mind,'' he said. ''Or tries to.''

''Well,'' Laura said, ''it's got a lot to learn about women.''

The director nodded. ''No doubt. You're the first woman it's communicated with that wasn't a scientist.''

''It's not so hot with security ops either,'' I said.

''To adjust,'' Sass said, ''the receiver must first have a mind.''

''I'll buy one first chance I get,'' I assured him. ''Anything to please that dumb hunk of rock.''

CHAPTER 5

"So far, it's kind of routine," I said. "If you forget we're in another dimension and there's a war on."

We were seated in a spacious suite that the director had assigned to us. I poured Laura another shot of what passed for a euphoric in these parts. It was bright, clear orange, and if you had enough of it, you even got to like war, if not actually want to fight in one. Judging by the way I felt, the juice still had a way to go.

Sass took a pull on his beverage, sighed contentedly. The sigh of someone who was about to powder out. "You don't seem to realize, Dunjer, if things go well here and you unmask the spy, it may be the beginning of an unprecedented trade agreement between Happy City and Magalone. And, of course, Security Plus would no doubt snare a permanent contract to safeguard the nation against its enemies.''

"Given the director's personality," I said, "the UI might not be the only ones. Thing is, even the mechs aren't too keen on being blown to bits in some stupid fracas.''

Sass squirmed irritably in his chair, glared at me. "Cold war, Dunjer, *cold* as an ice cube," he said. "So tell me, what is your strategy?''

"It's really the director's," I said. "I'm supposed to be the field exec of something called Robotics, Inc. Laura's my sidekick. And the mechs are our charges.''

"Where do we come from?" Laura asked. "Some other state?''

"Uh uh. Here in Magalone, Trex says.''

"They'll buy that?''

"Why not?" Sass said. "This is a country, not a city-state.''

I nodded. "A big country. We're from the east coast, which is like another world, they tell me.''

"What kind of world?" Laura asked.

"Trex is digging up some hypno-sleep discs on the topic. We'll know more than the natives come morning.''

She nodded. "And the mechs are to be manuals?''

"Yeah." I grinned. "They'll love that. Nothing but high-class floor sweeps, porters, and janitors. Once the staff gets used to seeing a bunch of metal men clanging around, they'll become as conspicuous as ashtrays or pencil sharpeners. No one'll pay 'em the least attention. And they'll have the run of the place. Each one of those babies is a walking arsenal of spy gadgets. No one'll be safe, not even us.''

Sass put down his empty glass, got to his feet. "Well,

then, if that is settled, I will be heading home." He fished around in a pocket, came up holding two small cubes, handed one to each of us. "If there is some emergency, merely signal with this, and I will come to your immediate rescue."

"You got it wrong, pal. It's I who always rescues you."

"That is becoming very monotonous," he said. "It is definitely time for a change."

"I'm sure we won't need to be rescued," Laura said.

"Yeah, what could happen?" I said. "As long as the dumb Ul remember it's a *cold* war, eh, Sass?"

"You will thank me, Dunjer, when you are wallowing in the director's generous fee."

"I'll be too busy wallowing. Besides, I've already thanked you. And, anyway, your huge finder's fee should be thanks enough."

"Actually, it is. I shall drop by in a few days," Sass said, "to check on your progress. Bye."

"Toodles," I said.

He blinked out.

"We really in another dimension?" Laura asked.

"That's what he says."

"What does that mean?"

"Damned if I know," I said.

CHAPTER 6

I sat perched on a gunmetal gray desk in a far corner
of the director's lab and eyed the hectic activity going
on around me. A couple of hundred people were busy
at the large computer that was part of Trex's Destabilizer.
Other staff members kept popping up through various
side doors and the lift. Everyone seemed frantic, as if
last night's layoff in my honor had put a permanent crimp
in their schedule.

I reached for the oversized mug behind me, took a
swig of good old Happy City coffee. I'd brought along
a three-week supply, more than I or Laura would ever
need if the job went smoothly. Sass wasn't the only one
who could think big. I was hoping to get some of the
natives hooked on the stuff and put Security Plus into
the export game. If crime ever slumped in Happy City,

we could all fall back on coffee. Especially if it were in its liquid state and we were in bathing suits.

"Remember to use filters for the best in flavor," an annoying voice murmured in my head.

"How would *you* know?" I asked the Crystal.

"From your mind."

"If it's in my mind I know it already," I pointed out with blinding clarity. "Why don't you pester some of the staff?"

"I'm doing that, too. Only they consider my presence a veritable blessing."

"It takes all kinds."

"I find your mind very interesting. If rather primitive."

"Beat it. Before I tell the boss."

"It won't do any good. He likes me."

"Another word, pal, I abandon this world to the Ul. They'll turn you into a mound of rubble. Scat."

It went.

Leaving the field to the stupid hypno-disk. "Clear and beautiful Lake Waggonea nestled between Mt. Stribbens and Calisgo Valley," a syrupy voice rattled around in my noggin, "is but a stone's throw from Greechi, the teeming metropolis of Magalone's east coast."

"Jeez," I said.

"No, Kriltz," a fat man in a white lab jacket said. "Who is this Jeez; he works here?"

"Forget it," I said.

"And you are the man with the mechanicals?"

"Uh huh."

"I am Kriltz," he said.

"Yeah, I know. Dunjer's the name."

"That is a very peculiar name," he said. "Uncommon. Kriltz is a dime a dozen. They have many Dunjers on the east coast?"

"A couple."

"From where on the east coast are you?"

"Clear and beautiful Lake Waggonea," I said.

"Is that not a resort area?"

"Yeah, I go there from Greechi, the teeming metropolis."

"Ah, Greechi."

"It's only a stone's throw away," I said. "Here, try some of this."

I reached behind me for the thermos, poured him a cup of coffee.

He eyed it suspiciously. "It is black."

"Uh huh."

"What is it?"

"It's called coffee."

"What?"

"It's all the rage on the east coast."

I handed him the cup. He sniffed at it, took a swallow. "Very bad," he said.

"Yeah, we east coasters are big on self-abuse."

He went away.

A lady came by. "Coffee, ma'am?"

"What is it?"

"An east coast taste delight."

"The east coast is a den of iniquity."

She went. A tall, skinny guy hurried by carrying a clipboard.

" 'Scuse me, sir. Try some coffee?"

"Is it an intoxicant?"

"No, it's quite harmless."

"Not interested." He scrammed.

XX41 came over. "Are you sure there's no war on?"

"Why do you ask?"

"If you'd go to the very end of town, you'd know."

I shook my head. "You think I'm sitting here just to get a load off my feet, don't you, XX41? Shirking duty. Letting others work while I while away the time. Well, you couldn't be more wrong. What I'm really doing is casing the personnel here. And also, at the very same time, building a vast coffee empire. You'll have to take it on faith, kid. You'll understand all this high-class security stuff a bit better when you grow older and mature."

"Mechs don't mature, skipper; when they grow older they just rust."

"So they do, XX41. Before that happens, why don't you tell me what you saw."

"Soldiers, chief, thousands of soldiers dug in at the edge of the dome."

"Were they shooting?"

"Uh uh."

"Then it's not war, merely a wise defensive measure to prevent war and justify the military budget. Read your history books."

"I'll leave that to you, boss."

"Actually, that's the assignment I always give to the junior clerk's assistant. How are the mechs doing?"

"They've got this place swept, mopped, and waxed, boss, but so far they haven't turned up any spies."

"Well, if there aren't any spies, they won't be able to say we didn't do *anything*."

"We?"

"Remember the empire, kid."

It went.

A short man with sharp features, slicked back shiny black hair, and a slight paunch came over. He wore a gray, high collared belted jacket, sharply creased gray slacks, and gleaming black boots.

"Coffee?" I said "It's the latest thing."

"*You're* the latest thing," he said. "You and those damn mechanicals."

"You don't like the noble metal men?"

"Not prowling around I don't. I'm Guver, State Security."

"I'm Dunjer, household mechs. 'Let a strong metal hand do your chores for you.' That's our motto. What've you got against 'em prowling around?"

"No security clearance, that's what. The director went over my head on this one."

"To your boss?"

"To himself. He's the big boss, you know; can make any policy decision he wants. I was against it from the start."

I gave him a shrug and a smile. "Surely you do not fear the empty-headed addle-brained automaton, whose only ambition is to rid his immediate area of dirt and grime or haul gigantic objects from one place to another. The innocent household mechanical is not the one to fear, my friend. *I* and my sidekick are the ones to fear. And the old director checked us out personally."

Guver waved his hand. "What does *he* know? Did he go to State Security School? Did he study Eavesdropping, Shadowing, Obtaining the Timely Confession, or even the Proper Use of the Truncheon? Did he?"

"I sure hope not, pal."

"All he knows is how to override State Security."

"That and a bit of science, eh?"

34

Guver fixed me with a cold gray eye. "Science is the handmaiden of the state, and State Security is its foundation."

He turned on his heel, marched off.

I wondered how his slogan would look on a Security Plus letterhead. Not too hot, I figured.

I refilled my mug.

"How you doing, kiddo?" Laura asked, coming up behind me.

"Holding my own," I said. "Which is more than can be said for this dumb product I've been trying to peddle."

"Still on the coffee empire kick, are you?"

"Look," I said, "once you've nabbed your spy, that's it, the game's over. But get someone drinking coffee and it's a going concern. Damn stuff's addictive."

"What happened to your love of humanity, Thomas?"

"Hey, it's coffee, not dope."

"Spot anything suspicious?"

"Yeah, everyone."

"The coffee has gone to your brain."

"If I didn't know any better," I complained, "I'd think we were still back in Happy City."

CHAPTER 7

"Whaddya mean we haven't traced it yet?" I asked. "We're supposed to be able to trace anything."

"It's a low-frequency signal," Laura said.

"So?"

"It's diffused, skipper," XX41 said. "A nefarious scheme to bemuse us. So far, they've succeeded. You don't think they have our number, do you?"

"How could they? Our number's in another dimension."

"They're using a wide beam," Laura said patiently. "It could be coming from anywhere."

The three of us were huddled in a small room off the main lab. It was early afternoon. I took a bite of my sandwich, a genuine Magalonian home-grown article. It tasted all right, but I was afraid to ask what was in it.

Not that I'd know if they told me.

"Coming from *anywhere*?" I said.

"Either from here in the science complex," she said, "or out there in the city."

"Still under the dome, eh?"

"Right," she said. "And the beam appears to be aimed out into Ul territory."

"Strictly forbidden," XX41 said primly. "There are posters everywhere. Right next to the no spitting, swearing, and criticizing the government posters."

"Yeah," I said, polishing off my sandwich. "If you know it's forbidden, XX41, the denizens around here do too. Good. That means the bad guys are up to something."

"What's good about it, chief?" XX41 asked. "We rooting for the other side?"

"Not yet," I said. "They haven't come up with an offer yet."

"Don't take him seriously, XX41," Laura said. "That's what humans call a joke."

"I thought it was just good business sense," XX41 said.

"Of course there are spies here," Trex said, glowering at me as though I'd dared to criticize the government despite the poster warnings. "How could you ever have doubted it? No self-respecting adversary would be without them."

"Well, it could be some birdbrained ham, broadcasting just for the hell of it."

I was in the director's office, seated in an armchair. Trex was behind his desk. I had dragged him here for a quiet chat away from prying ears.

"You are doing what, if I may ask?"

"The usual high-tech security stuff. I've got some mechs adjusting our receivers right now. We've almost zeroed in."

The director nodded thoughtfully. "I'll alert Guver at once."

"I wouldn't do that," I said. "We don't know who might be involved. State Security could be leaking like a sieve for all we know."

"It is airtight. Guver himself oversees the clearance procedure."

"And who oversees him?"

"There is no need to oversee him."

"Maybe. You ought to have the Crystal give him the once-over, anyway. Damn thing crawls right in your mind and starts snooping around. At least you could put it to good use."

"Has it been annoying you?"

"Yeah, you might say that."

"I'm sorry," Trex said. "The Knowledge Crystal does become a bit playful at times." He reached into a drawer, removed something that looked like a gold coin, held it out to me.

"Kind of early for my fee, isn't it?"

"Not payment, Mr. Dunjer. This is an inhibitor. Most of us carry one. It keeps the Crystal from probing one's mind."

I rose, took the object, studied it. "Still looks like a coin to me."

"It is." Trex smiled. "Merely one of the many natural substances that blocks the Crystal."

"That why you don't use him for security?"

He nodded. "The Knowledge Crystal has many uses,

but intelligence work isn't one of them. There are also artificial means of blocking him. As well as ways to traduce him into reporting false thoughts.''

I pocketed the coin. "I'll miss the rascal," I said. "But not much."

"Could be anywhere in Happy City," I said, glancing out the car window, "if you go by appearances."

"And if they put a dome over it," XX41 said.

We were driving through the capital of Magalone. Metal and glass towers were on either side of us. Elevated speedways rose over and around the buildings. Mechs filled our car. More mechs were in a vehicle up front. Still more in cars on side streets. Laura and I were along for the human angle, but mostly this was a mech mission.

"North," a mech voice said through the communo beeper.

We tuned north at the next corner, wheeled along at a pretty good clip.

The towers began to change height and exteriors, grew smaller as we approached the beginning of a residential section.

"Northeast," another mech voice beeped us.

We turned at the next intersection. I gazed through the window at what looked like a shopping mall. I wondered if I'd have time to do some bargain hunting around here. If Laura and I hopped off now, no one would be the wiser. The mechs could mop up the spies, and I could collect the fee. Unless, of course, something unlikely happened and the spies mopped up the mechs. Then, it was vital that I be along. Mainly to think up the right excuse. Some things you just didn't want to entrust to a mech.

"Due east," a voice spoke through the communo.

We swerved at the corner, headed east. Houses still flashed by outside. Our tech mech had fiddled with our standard homing gear, fine-tuned it to the low-frequency signal in jig time, give or take a step. A three-car vise was drawing tighter around the broadcasters. Two other cars were packed with fighter mechs. Trex had made us special lawmen for the occasion, given us badges bearing the director's seal. The bad guys wouldn't be impressed, but it would look better in court, no doubt—provided they had courts around here.

"I wonder," Laura said, "why they picked this time to break radio silence?"

"Who knows? Maybe they became lonesome for some genuine Ul small talk."

"You'll be able to ask them in a minute, boss," XX41 said. "We're almost there."

CHAPTER 8

We stopped in sight of our destination—a full block away—and waited. The rest of our troop was circling around, hemming in the enemy.

We'd left the swankier houses behind. Here the sparse structures were mostly two story wood or concrete. Scraggly trees and foliage separated one house from the next. I figured this was where the servants holed up, the ones who tended to the folks in the towers and town houses we'd passed. They'd have reason enough to snitch on their betters if this was the best Magalone could do for them. Not that Happy City was any different.

The house we wanted wasn't much better than a glorified shack. Crooked, unpainted planks made up its exterior. A weed garden surrounded it. The weeds weren't the only ones.

"Okay," a mech voice beeped us. "We're set."

"Now what?" Laura asked.

I looked at XX41. It, Laura, and I were the only ones left in the car. "You going to lead the charge from here?" I asked.

"Me?"

"You."

"I thought you would reserve that privilege for yourself, skipper."

"One of your circuits must be faulty."

"You really want me to get out there, chief?"

"Yeah. You can cower behind a tree if you want. We need to know what's cooking from close up."

"And you, boss?"

"I and Miss Fallsom will cower here in the car."

The mech climbed out, shot us both a look as if awaiting a recall. Or maybe a physical to determine if it were fit for the unreasonable duty I'd assigned it.

"Good luck, pal," I said.

"We who are about to die—"

"Vamoose," I said.

It went.

"There goes a brave gladiator," Laura said.

"Don't you believe it."

"Thomas, we're really just going to sit here?"

"Uh huh. Unless there's shooting. Then we get down flat on the floor. You gotta understand one thing, sweetie: the essence of field work is staying alive so you can get to the next field. We can always give XX41 a new arm or leg if one gets shot off. But, for us, they might not even have a limb bank on this world. Besides, I'm kind of attached to the ones I've got. And yours are even nicer."

"What if XX41 is hit in the head?"

"Don't be carried away by wishful thinking."

"Ready," a mech voice said over the communo.

"Go," I said staunchly. My one contribution to the day's proceedings. I was glad my sidekick was there to note it.

Metal men descended on the house from four sides, a veritable onslaught of hardware. As if shoehorns, hammers, and thumbtacks had suddenly taken on a life of their own. No bullhorns urged the inhabitants to give themselves up. No warnings were sounded. The less time the beamers had for heroics, the quicker we could fold the operation.

Someone must have been posted at one of the windows. A few shots rang out. The mechs didn't seem to mind. They went right through the walls. An inspiring sight—especially for anyone who held stock in my outfit.

A moment passed in silence as the pair of us stared at the now ruined shack.

I said, "Don't let the excitement get you, kiddo."

"Some excitement."

My beeper beeped. "All clear," it said.

"They disarmed?" I asked.

"Why bother? The sight of the noble mechanicals has left them virtually paralyzed," XX41 said through the communo. I could see him behind his tree, not too far off.

"How would *you* know?"

"It always does, skipper."

"He's right," a mech voice said through the communo. "But we disarmed them anyway, just in case."

"Good thinking," I said, as Laura and I climbed out of the car.

Three guys were in the house. Along with a dozen mechs. The guys, all in shirt sleeves and dark trousers, didn't look any too pleased.

"What is the meaning of this?" a short, stocky man with a graying beard demanded. "Why have these robots broken into my home?"

"Because you were using a hidden transmitter," I said.

"They don't like hidden transmitters?" he asked.

"They can take 'em or leave 'em," I said. "It's *I* who don't like 'em."

"And who are you?"

I flashed the seal. "The law," I said with simple dignity.

The man looked disgusted. "Where were you," he demanded, "when I was being robbed on the subway last week?"

"Wrong type of law, pal."

"Traffic cop?"

"Intelligence unit."

"They don't look very intelligent," he said, nodding toward the mechs. "You don't, either. *She* looks smart."

"Thank you," Laura said.

"The transmitter's here in the other room, skipper," XX41 called.

"You may look smart with that beard, pal," I said, "but you got caught anyway. So much for mere looks."

"What's the use?" the shortest of the three man spoke up, wringing his hands. "They've got us dead to rights." He was a young guy with red curly hair.

"Shut up!" the third one hollered. He had a bald head, handlebar mustache, and piercing brown eyes. A suspicious enough character even under the best of circumstances. Which these certainly weren't.

The short one turned on him. "Haven't you done enough?"

"Enough or not," I said, "it's all over. Come clean and maybe we'll go easy on you." And then again, maybe not. I kept this last bit of conjecture to myself. No need depressing these lads any more than necessary.

"It was all his idea," the redhead said, wagging his thumb at baldy.

The guy with the beard disagreed. "We're all equally responsible, Argick." I figured Argick was the redhead's name and not some exclamation denoting guilt. But I wouldn't have bet my life on it.

"You admit trying to contact the Ul?" Laura asked.

"What do you mean trying?" bald head sneered. "We have been broadcasting to them all afternoon!"

"How many of you are there?" I asked.

"You can't count?" bald head said.

"That's it, eh, a three-man spy ring?" I didn't bother keeping the skepticism out of my voice.

"*He's* the only spy," the redhead said, nodding at bald head.

Bald head snapped to attention. "Every man in his place!" he shouted.

"What's that?" I asked. "The password?"

"The Ul motto," the bearded one said. "Don't you know?"

"They make us lead sheltered lives in Intelligence," I explained, "so we can concentrate on the main task. Nabbing guys like you."

"Him, not us," the redhead said.

"He want's war," the bearded one said.

"For a greater Ul!" the bald guy shouted.

"But we," the bearded one said, "are trying to stop war."

"War is glory!" the bald guy yelled.

"He yells again," I told the nearest mech, "bop him over the noodle."

"Aye, aye, chief."

"But they wouldn't listen to us," the redhead said.

"The Ul?" Laura said.

"The Ul," the redhead said.

"Now it's too late," the bearded one said.

"Quite right," XX41 said. "We've turned off the transmitter."

"It was too late even before that," the redhead said. "The Ul heard us out."

"But they drew the wrong conclusions," the bearded one said.

Bald head smiled evilly. "The *right* conclusions." He glared at me. "I used these two, had them in the palm of my hand, told them what they wished to hear." He chuckled. "And they served the Ul, gave them what they needed to know. Now there will be war."

The redhead looked ashen. "He's right, of course; there will be war."

"What did you give them?" I asked.

Bald head laughed. "The secret of the Destabilizer," he said, "what else?"

CHAPTER 9

"Nonsense," Trex snorted.

Laura and I were seated in the director's office. It was still devoid of furnishings, but I didn't expect to be around long enough to mind.

"They seemed to think," Laura said, "that they'd handed over your top secret weapon to the enemy."

A thin smile played across the director's face. "The Destabilizer is still being perfected. Even I have not fathomed its full potentialities."

"Forget about its potentialities," I said. "Is there a blueprint those guys could've swiped?"

"Nothing that would do them any good," Trex said. He tapped his skull with a bony forefinger.

"It's in your head, eh?"

He gave me a thin smile. "And that, as you can see,

is still firmly attached." A mech couldn't have sounded prouder of the fact.

"So what did those jokers think they were getting?" I demanded.

Trex shrugged. "Bits and pieces, at best. Bluch and Argick are data specialists. They work with that part of the Destabilizer that is the computer, feed it data."

"What's the other part?" Laura asked.

Trex's eyes gleamed. "The weapon."

"Yeah," I said. "The mere thought gives me a warm, glowy feeling, too. But if you know one part, don't you also know the other?"

Trex looked impatient. "Of course not. It is all compartmentalized. The left hand never knows what the right is doing. Only I and the Knowledge Crystal have the complete picture."

"Any chance the Crystal blabbed?"

"None whatsoever. It speaks of these matters only to me." The director actually smirked. "That is why the claims of those two," he said, "are so preposterous."

"What about the third guy?" I asked. "The one with the bald head?"

"Maintenance," Trex said.

Laura raised an eyebrow. "Of the weapon?"

"The building," Trex said. "Litsh was the janitor." I nodded. "Had the run of this place?"

"Of course. How else could he perform his duties?"

"An okay cover," I said. "The shack where they stashed the transmitter was his?"

"Bluch's," Trex said.

"Jeez, no wonder the guy was a spy," I said. "You don't pay beans for high-class techs, do you?"

"There's a war on," Trex said.

"Cold war," I reminded him. "That's the part we signed on for. And by the looks of things, we may have wrapped up our end of the deal."

"We'll see about that," the director said. He touched a button on his desk.

Almost at once, the door popped open, and Guver, the State Security chief, stepped into the room, snapped to attention, and saluted.

Trex nodded casually and the chief unwound. Just in time. Watching him was giving me muscle strain.

"You keep him at the door," Laura asked, "like some poodle?"

"His office," Trex said coldly, "is down the hall."

The little man's paunch, I saw, was still protruding, and his black hair was still slicked back, but the gray, belted jacket had been swapped for a black, high-collared uniform. The belt, this time, was leather, and a long, black holster hung from it. He turned his sharp-featured face my way. "The household mechs man, I see."

Let a strong metal hand do your chores for you, I thought. But had enough sense to keep the advice to myself.

"I felt it best," the director said, "that Mr. Dunjer and his team work under complete cover."

Guver strode to the center of the room. "If the director has lost confidence in me, I gladly offer my resignation."

"Try not to be an ass, Guver," Trex said. "If I had lost confidence in you, I'd have had you shot. Now, what about the prisoners?"

"They have all confessed."

Trex nodded. "Naturally. They always do."

"They confessed a number of times," Guver said.

"And were the confessions always the same?" Trex

asked, leaning forward at his desk.

"Always."

"Ah." He sat back in his seat. "A sure sign of veracity." To me he said, "We employ the most scientific methods when extracting confessions."

"Yeah, your boy here mentioned a few. They in it alone, Guver?"

"Must I answer this man's questions?"

"We're all on the same team," I said brightly.

"Answer," Trex said.

"They appear to have acted alone." His gray eyes bored into me as if daring me to challenge his assertion. "We have computer printouts on all their friends and associates," he continued in a rush. "We shall be doing a round-the-clock security check on them. The transmitter seems to be their sole means of communicating with the enemy. Our monitors were unable to detect the beam." Guver seemed to choke on that last bit, but, pro that he was, managed to get it out.

"Baldy said he was the real spy," I said.

"He was."

"He tricked the others into helping him?"

"He did."

"What kind of tricks—magic or money?"

"Words."

"That's the worst of all. What words?"

"That giving our military secrets to the enemy would show them the futility of attacking Magalone."

"Not a bad argument," I said, "especially if you're a birdbrain. They responsible for the sabotage, too?"

"Only Litch. He was a trained agent."

"Beats being a janitor," I said.

"Unless you're caught," Laura said.

"When will you have a complete report for me?" Trex wanted to know.

"Within forty-eight hours."

"Very well." He nodded.

Guver snapped to attention, saluted, turned on his heel, and left.

"Why do I think that guy doesn't like me?" I asked.

Trex sighed. "You have encroached on his territory, Mr. Dunjer, that is why."

"As long as it's not my personality," I said.

"He doesn't know you well enough," Laura said sweetly, "to take offense. Unlike the rest of us."

"Guy didn't seem too keen on you either, kiddo," I pointed out.

The director shook his head. "I am surrounded by prima donnas. Surely you will spare me?"

"Yeah, I show mercy for my clients."

"Almost ex-client," Trex said happily. "It does look as if your job is done."

"So it does," I said.

"Really a cut-and-dried operation," Laura said.

"All it took," I said, "was a smidgen of high-tech know-how. Which is, after all, our specialty."

"Then all that remains is to compute your bill."

"Something like that. But as long as we're here, we might as well hang around a bit."

"I fail to follow," Trex said.

"Finish mopping up."

"I thought you had."

"With mop and pail. The cleanup job. When Security Plus starts something, they like to finish."

* * *

I held the monitor cube up in the air, did a complete circle of the room.

"Clean," I said. "They must be slipping."

"Why," XX41 asked, "should they plant bugs in the laundry room?"

"Why not?" I said. "They've bugged everything else."

The whole crew was gathered in the laundry room. Mechs stood shoulder to shoulder with their blood brothers, washing machines and dryers. The place didn't smell much different than a Happy City laundromat. Detergent was probably the universal solvent, the one thing that never changed even when you switched universes. It was not an uplifting thought.

"X5," I said, "stand by the door. Anyone wants to come in, tell 'em the machines are all taken."

X5 moved to his post.

"Report, guys" I said.

"There are hundreds of bugs in this city," X9 said, "if not thousands. Many are the standard type, but some are quite advanced, and no doubt considered undetectable on this world. These are, of course, the ones that received our greatest attention. Some of them, I might add, seemed quite legitimate."

"True enough," X32 said. "It is doubtless important to gauge the morale of the military. Which must be why all the barracks are bugged."

"Doubtless," I said.

"Along with the strategy room," X9 said.

"Of course," X32 said, "generals are part of the military. And deserve as much attention as the rest."

Laura turned to me. "Are they kidding?"

"Kidding sounds about right," I said. "As far as the

delivery goes. Our mechs would never fudge the facts. Would you guys?''

"Never," X32 agreed.

"The laboratory is bugged," X12 said. "I was mopping up in there and had no trouble finding the devices. Especially since I am electronically designed to do so. Some bugs are planted in the computer itself. And one was embedded in the Knowledge Crystal."

"There are," X22 said, "three bugs in the director's office. One in the ceiling and one in his communo."

"Where's the third one?" I asked.

"In the john. I hesitate to mention it in mixed company."

"How quaint," Laura said.

"It means mechs and humans," I said.

"The chief scientists on the director's staff are also bugged," X4 said. "Both in their offices and homes."

"How about State Security?" I wanted to know.

"They have an entire floor to themselves in this building," X31 said. "It is free of listening devices."

"What about their own building?" I asked. State Security had a tower out in the domed city. Trex had given my household mechs a special pass so they could estimate cleaning costs.

"I went through it, boss," X27 said. "Some of their computers were almost smart enough to note my monitor gear. But not quite. The tower contains no bugs."

"Anything of interest?" I asked.

"A computer," X27 said, "whose sole function is to process bugging data."

"From where?"

"All the bugs found by my colleagues."

"All, eh?"

"And lots of others."

"Must keep the old computer pretty busy," I said.

"It offered no greeting. But one can't really fault this apparent lapse in manners. The computer had a room of its own in the subbasement, behind heavy metal magnolocked doors. I was unable to approach it. I was shielded, of course, so my sensor probes would go undetected."

"Uh huh. Is this data automatically relayed elsewhere?"

"No. It remains in the data bank until manually called up."

"Anyone do that little thing?"

"Not yet, boss."

"X27, displaying the keen intelligence and dexterity for which the noble mechanical is justly famous," XX41 said, "sequestered a spy cube on the premises."

"You X27's agent?" I asked.

"It's a thought," XX41 said. "The spy cube is being monitored. When the data's retrieved we'll be able to follow it to its destination."

"That will be Guver," Laura said.

"Maybe," I said.

"He's Security chief," Laura said.

"Yeah, but it could be one of his underlings."

"I sure hope not."

"You're not the only one."

"I am not fond of the man, Thomas."

"But that's the test, isn't it, sweetie?"

"It is?"

"Sure. Of our professional objectivity."

"I didn't know we had any."

"It's built into the mechs, honey; we can't wiggle out of it without looking rotten. Besides, we won't be here long enough to frame the guy. And anyway, he's probably guilty."

"Got it all figured out, haven't you?"

"Yeah, if I don't, XX41 does, and why should it get the credit?"

"So we wait for someone to retrieve the data, follow that someone to his source, and nab Guver."

"Yeah, especially if it is Guver. I'm keeping my fingers crossed."

"He won't catch on?"

"Uh uh. Because our high tech really *is* superior. Every once in a while our ad boys tell the truth. And this is one of those whiles."

CHAPTER **10**

"The trouble is," I said, "they're not up to the good old Happy City standard."

Laura put her hands on her hips, gazed into the full-length mirror. She had on a clinging, almost transparent, purple dress with a pastel flower pattern.

"And the good old Happy City standard," I continued, "is no great shakes to begin with."

"Besides," Laura said, "back home they'd arrest me for wearing this thing on the street."

"Hmmmm," I said, thoughtfully. "Maybe you *should* buy it."

"Won't last a season, Thomas. Material's too chintzy."

"Remember, there's a war on."

"Cold war. Though we should have gotten it in writing just to make sure."

She marched off to the dressing room.

We were in a large shopping mart a few blocks from the director's lab. I sat down on a handy bench, ogled the lady customers. Chintzy or not, there was something to be said for the way they made dresses on this world: it left little to the imagination. And for a guy like me who used up most of his imagination on tough security problems, that was a real plus.

Presently, Laura reclaimed me and we ambled off to take in the rest of the mart. Some forty-five minutes later my beeper beeped.

"Skipper," XX41 said, "something funny's going on."

"As in slapstick?"

"As in cloak and dagger. The word hat rack is being bandied about."

"Probably by people with hats."

"On a shielded beam?"

"Closet hat wearers. Get a fix on it?"

"It's coming from the State Security building, chief."

"And where's it going?"

"Throughout the city."

"Any other words?"

"Just that."

"Okay," I said, "I'll be back in a jiffy. Sit tight."

"As you know, sitting or standing is all the same to the noble mechanical."

"Yeah, I know; it just slipped my mind."

I beeped off.

"What do you make of it, Thomas?" Laura asked.

"Very cryptic. Maybe someone in State Security has flipped his cork. Then, again, maybe they're up to something."

She took my arm and we headed for an exit. "Lucky for us if they are," she said.

"Darn right. We catch 'em in the act, we'll probably pull down the Magalonian public service medal." I thought it over. "We melt that down, along with the coin and badge, and maybe we got ourselves a nice bonus."

"You're always thinking on your feet, aren't you, kiddo?"

"Yeah, especially when I can't find a nice easy chair," I said.

Things were buzzing in the laboratory, as usual. I made my way through small knots of scientists and techs. No one paid any attention to me. The household mech salesman had ceased to be a novelty. I reached the director's desk. He was going over a batch of computer printouts.

"Got a moment to spare?" I said.

Trex glanced up at me absently, the sheaf of papers still in his hand. "Ah, ready to go, are you? You'll be wanting your payment, of course."

"Not really."

"You won't be wanting your payment?"

"The 'not really' was for the first part. I'm not ready to go."

"Your mechs still tidying up?"

"Uh uh."

The director lowered the papers to the desk. I'd finally gotten his attention. Some of it, at least. "I don't understand," he said.

"I'd like to speak to you privately."

"I'm really quite busy at the moment, Mr. Dunjer."

"It's important," I said.

The director looked around. "No one is in earshot. Whatever you have to tell me will remain between us." He lowered his voice. "What is it, Mr. Dunjer, your crew find some spot that won't come clean?" Trex chuckled.

"Yeah," I said, "we found a real dirty spot. But it's too embarrassing to mention with all these people around. Maybe I'd just better show you, eh?"

Trex stared at me as if I'd asked him to waltz me around the lab. "Are you feeling quite well?"

"Sure, except for a touch of lumbago every now and then. Why not humor me; it's not every day you get a visitor from another dimension, is it?"

"Employee, not visitor." The director pushed back his chair, got reluctantly to his feet. "Where are we going?"

"The laundry room," I told him.

"It looks perfectly clean," he said.

"Nothing's perfect."

Trex peered behind a washing machine. "Clean here too. You haven't taken leave of your senses, have you, Mr. Dunjer?"

"Not any more than usual."

"Then why are we here?"

"Because this is one of the few spots in the building that isn't bugged."

"Bugged?"

"Yeah. As in 'loaded with listening devices.'"

The director stared at me incredulously. "You didn't tell me."

"Where should I tell you? In the lab? Your office? The hallway? All bugged."

"All?"

"Yeah, along with half your city."

"But that's dreadful."

"Depends on what side you're on, I'd imagine. I could've spilled the beans sooner, but it makes more sense to nail the perps first."

"You have done that?"

"We were about to do that."

"Were."

"That's the significant word, all right," I said. "The bugs all lead to the State Security building. So there's a real question just how secure your state is at the moment. A special computer's been set up in their basement to handle the data. We planted a spy cube that would tell us who was receiving this windfall. And that would've wrapped the whole thing up."

"What happened?"

"Hat rack."

"Uh?"

"Yeah, that's what I said too. It's a code word, Director Trex, being beamed from the State Security building; it's going through the city right now."

He shrugged. "State Security uses code words all the time. That is part of their function."

"How about bugging your office and home, that their function, too?"

"Of course not."

"It's the same shielded wavelength."

"The same."

"I think you're actually getting the picture, Trex. Congratulations."

He nodded. "I must contact Guver at once."

"Then again, maybe you're not. Listen, pal, Guver's the top guy there. Odds have it he's behind all this. Or one of his aides. Either way, he's compromised."

Trex shook his head. "I will never believe Guver is involved."

"Never is a long time. Look, I don't want to knock my peerless organization—the mechs wouldn't stand for it. But your State Security is a pretty sophisticated outfit, too. Ever wonder why they weren't able to turn up the bad guys?"

Trex wheeled on his heel, headed out the door. "Guver will have an explanation."

"Yeah, probably because he *is* the bad guys. Then it won't be an explanation you'll want to hear."

"What do you mean he's not there?" Trex said into the communo. He listened a moment. "Find him," he barked and rang off.

"Guy's lost, eh?" I asked.

"Off somewhere on a mission."

"Admirable devotion to duty," I said.

"Well, we don't keep him chained to this building."

"That's your mistake."

We were back in the director's office, Trex behind his desk. The desktop wasn't quite bare anymore: two deactivated bugs lay there. I'd pulled them first thing when we hit the office. So far, if Guver was the enemy, he hadn't missed much, since the call had been to him.

"This tips our hand," I said. "They'll know we're onto 'em."

He looked from me to the bugs. "So what do you suggest?"

"Put a few army units on alert, have 'em standing by. It can't hurt."

"You actually suspect," Trex said, "there are that many conspirators?"

"Even more maybe. What they won't know is whether we've stumbled across these two bugs or are really onto something. They'll go running to their computer, hoping for enlightenment. And that's when we'll find out who they are. And how many of them we've got to worry about. And maybe even what they intend to do about it."

"You make it sound easy."

"Nothing's easy," I said. "But my outfit does have a bit of expertise in these matters."

"I should certainly hope so."

"Hope and my mechs will see you through—if not exactly in that order. Don't worry, I'll take steps to cover any and all contingencies. This may actually be the break we've been waiting for."

CHAPTER 11

"Frankly, Thomas, I feel like a sitting duck," Laura whispered.

"Right. That's the trouble with being in the field," I whispered back. "It's open season on ops. Every lunatic feels free to take a potshot at you." I considered the matter. "Lunatics aren't half bad, really; they miss a lot. It's the sane guys you gotta watch out for."

"But you've managed to survive, battered and broken down as you are."

"True," I admitted. "As president of our hotshot firm, I get to sit behind a desk most times. And whenever I'm dragged into the field, I take along a bunch of mechs to hide behind. Just like now. Don't sweat it, honey, old broken down Tom wouldn't give you a bum steer. We're sitting pretty."

Nothing had changed in the big lab. Trex was back at his post. His staff was busy at their usual chores which I couldn't for the life of me begin to fathom, even if I'd wanted to. Laura and I were lounging in chairs near the center of the lab, with tall glasses in our hands, imbibing a mild local euphoric, which, judging by the way I felt, wasn't quite holding up its end. I wasn't so sure I was either, but I was giving it the old college try—right out of the *Ops Advanced Field Strategy Manual.* When in doubt, go by the book.

Two army units were on alert, so that I and my nifty sidekick wouldn't personally have to go down on the mat with the bad guys, a very important point. My mechs had been given their orders, an even more important point. I kept my ear cocked for my beeper. So far, it was mum. No one had been near the basement computer in State Security. I hoped these jokers had some other way of finding out a pair of their bugs had been discovered. Sometimes, it's a real pain keeping the opposition on schedule.

Laura took a swig of her beverage. "So if we're sitting pretty," she asked, "why are we whispering?"

"Because this place is still bugged, and we don't want the baddies to hear us."

"I knew that."

"Sure you did."

I took a sip of my euphoric.

"ATTENTION!" a voice said over a loudspeaker.

"Eh?" I said.

"YOUR LAB IS SURROUNDED," the voice said. "REMAIN WHERE YOU ARE. YOU WILL BE PROCESSED."

"Processed?" Laura said.

64

"It's something," I said, "they do to cheese, I think."

"Well," she said, "I don't want it done to me."

"Who would?" I beeped my beeper. "You get that, guys?"

"Every word, skipper."

"Edifying, eh?"

"It has renewed our vigor, chief."

"Don't let the processors hear that," I said. "They'll charge you extra."

I beeped off. "That's that," I said.

"*What's* that, kiddo?"

"We'll just have to see, won't we?"

We didn't have long to wait. In fact, less than a minute.

All the doors leading to the labs popped open at once, as if given a collective hotfoot.

"Company," I said cheerfully.

"About time," Laura said.

Black-clad security troops had begun pouring through the doors. They didn't look one bit friendly, as if they divined that in this very lab the state had somehow become insecure. These babies held a variety of weapons, were waving them around as if hunting for a convenient target. I was glad plenty of objects and people were between them and us.

"RESISTANCE IS FUTILE," the loudspeaker voice called.

It needn't have bothered. Resistance was the last thing on anyone's mind. Trex sat at his desk, looking thunderstruck. His scientists and techs were gaping at the intruders as if they were some kind of collective hallucination that might yet vanish. Good luck.

Slowly, the troops began to spread out against the walls, forming a circle around the laboratory. If anything, they looked sterner than ever. As if coming face-to-face with the scientists had convinced them of their wickedness.

Trex sprang to his feet. "What is the meaning of this?" he demanded. If he didn't know by now, he probably never would.

As if in answer the loudspeaker roared, "ATTENTION! THIS IS GENERAL GUVER. SUBVERSIVE ELEMENTS HAVE INFILTRATED THE DOME. THEIR SOLE AIM IS TO CREATE HAVOC BETWEEN MAGALONE AND ITS NEIGHBOR, UL. IN THIS CRISIS, I HAVE ASSUMED SUPREME COMMAND. PUBLIC SAFETY WILL BE MAINTAINED. THE ENEMIES OF THE STATE WILL BE UPROOTED. ALL POWER TO STATE SECURITY!"

"Doesn't beat around the bush," Laura whispered.

"Guy's really done it," I said with some wonder, "pulled all the stops."

"We prompted him to this rash act, Thomas?"

"Probably. I didn't know we had it in us."

Slowly, the troops began to edge forward, drawing the circle ever tighter around the lab. They kept their guns aimed at the crowd, as if afraid one of the scientists might suddenly invent a counterweapon.

"Those things shoot real bullets?" Laura asked.

"Yeah, bullets. Not lasers but bullets. That's an important distinction."

"This is no time for splitting hairs, Thomas. What do we do?"

"Duck."

Trex held up a hand. "This is treason!" he shouted. "Put down your weapons now and I promise you all leniency."

A trooper raised his gun, let loose a nice, ear-shattering blast over the director's head. "Silence!" he roared.

"A promise that's hard to resist," I said.

"But they managed."

"Shows character."

The techs and scientists had begun to back up, were being herded like cattle toward the center of the lab. Trex looked over in my direction, wrinkled his brow, all but shook his fist at me. As if somehow I were responsible for this latest calamity. I grinned back at him, shrugged. If he thought I was going to pull out my laser and take on the troops, he had another guess coming. Of course, I did have a surprise or two up my sleeve, but it wouldn't've been a surprise if I'd told him.

By now there was plenty of empty space between the troops and the doors. No doubt, guards had been posted in the corridors and stairwells. But these clowns had never come up against the intrepid metal men before.

Again, the doors all popped open at once, as though they'd learned a new trick they couldn't resist practicing. This time, a stream of mechs poured through the doorways. They carried no weapons in their hands. They *were* weapons.

"Drop your guns!" a chorus of mechs shouted in unison, forming a makeshift amplifying system.

Their command brought instant results.

The troops whirled around, ignoring their unarmed prisoners, who for the moment had ceased being targets. Score one for our side. Laura and I exchanged glances.

The first three lines of troops dropped to one knee and opened fire. Behind them, three rows of standing troops joined in. The racket alone was almost lethal.

But mechs aren't much bothered by mere bullets, are, in fact, impervious to them.

The mechs held out their arms as if to beseech their attackers.

Each pointed a finger as if in accusation.

Electricity crackled through the air, jumped from mechs to troops.

Screams took the place of shots, a far more satisfying sound. Guns fell from spastic fingers, clattered to the floor. The troops followed their weapons, keeled over, lay there twitching, as if their quiet snooze was being bedeviled by nightmares.

I smiled at Laura. "Didn't even work up a sweat."

"Mechs don't sweat."

"I meant *us*. Didn't get killed either, if you'll note. Must've done something right, eh?"

"That was the mechs again, kiddo."

I shrugged. "What we got 'em for, isn't it?"

I looked around at Trex and his bunch. The ones who hadn't frozen solid at the sound of gunfire were picking themselves off the floor. I waved at the director, gave him a cheery grin. He was busy wiping his brow with a large hanky. Some employers are the worrying kind.

I beeped my beeper.

"Skipper?" XX41 said uncertainly.

"Who else would it be?"

"Whoever took the beeper off your body."

"My body?"

"Well, nonmechs *are* mortal," it said. "Is the fighting over?"

"Uh huh. Short and sweet."

"Not out here it isn't."

"Where are you?"

"In the laundry room."

"There's fighting in the laundry room?"

"Out in the city. I've set up the monitors in the laundry room. Who would think of coming here during this terrible war?"

"War, yet. Better report, chum."

"There's fighting everywhere, chief. At least those places where we stashed the spy cubes. The security police and army are going at it tooth and nail."

"Who's winning?"

"Hard to tell, boss. But as there are more of the army then State Security, it's a good bet they'll come out ahead. Only don't bet the firm, chief; sometimes good bets have been known to come in dead last."

CHAPTER 12

I beeped off, looked around. The mechs were busy handcuffing their catch. None of the troopers objected; they were still exploring dreamland.

I nodded at Laura. We both rose, made our way to Trex. A small crowd had gathered around him, chattering away excitedly. We shoved our way through.

The director caught sight of me, opened his mouth either to complain or offer his congratulations. I cut him short.

"There's a war going on in your city," I told him. "Better get snapping, Trex, or even my mechs won't be able to bail you out."

Around us, all talk had stopped, as if the speakers had suddenly been struck mute. The folks in the rest of the lab, as if compensating for this deficiency, were making a fine din.

"Surely not the Ul?" Trex said.

"Their allies," Laura said.

The director looked puzzled, as though—despite all that had just happened—the mere thought of Ul allies was beyond his comprehension.

"Your State Security forces," Laura said.

"They're going toe-to-toe with the army," I told him. "They're busy raising hell right now."

The director's hazel eyes gazed at me and my blond-headed partner as if we were speaking in some secret op language only we could understand. The director was obviously in shock. "State Security?" he said stupidly.

"Yeah," I said. "The same bunch that are being cuffed by my mechs."

Trex's head swiveled slowly, as if turning on broken hinges, took in the scene. "But these are renegades."

"So are the rest of 'em."

"They were constantly monitored."

"By whom, Guver?"

He nodded slowly. As though his head had suddenly become a burden far too heavy to bear.

"Don't you get it, Trex?" I said. "Guver hasn't made his play with a handful of stooges, he's turned the whole ministry. They're trying to take over."

"The entire city's at risk," Laura said. "You've got to do something."

The director seemed to come awake with a start. His hand shot out, jabbed a button on his desk. A portion of the desktop slid back, revealing a communo and keyboard. A red light was blinking on and off.

"What's that?" I asked.

"Red alert."

"It didn't beep you?" Laura asked.

"I keep it turned off."

"Jeez," I said. "No wonder Guver was able to run circles around you."

"I have a staff to handle all this," Trex said testily, like his old lovable self. "My work here takes precedence."

"Your work," I pointed out, "will go down the tubes, along with you, if Guver pulls this off."

He gazed down at the keyboard, punched a key. Instantly, a voice came over the speaker.

"Director Trex?" it yelled hysterically.

"Yes."

"Thank heavens! This is Vice Director Srik. Are you all right, sir?"

"Yes, yes, perfectly."

"We feared the laboratory had been taken."

"What's going on, man?" Trex barked.

"The security forces are attempting a coup."

"*All* of them?"

"At least two thirds. The rest have either deserted or joined our ranks."

I broke in. "The enemy making any headway?"

"Who is that?" Srik demanded.

"Answer him!" Trex bawled into the communo.

"Yes, sir! Headway is not quite the word, sir," Srik said. "They have taken over the Defense Ministry and the communications network. They have been reinforced by units outside the dome. The east end of the city has been overrun. Other sections are completely cut off. They took us by surprise, sir. The administration building might have fallen too, but we were warned in time."

"Warned?" Laura asked.

"Who spoke?" Srik asked.

"Answer, by god!" Trex roared.

"Yes, sir! From the lab complex, sir. Someone with the title of household mech—whatever that is. Are you sure you're all right, sir?"

"Perfectly. And our army?"

"They have remained loyal, down to the last man."

"How they doing?" I asked.

"All units in the dome are engaging the enemy. General Frimz has summoned the Third Mobile Battalion from the Ul border. It will reach the dome within the hour."

"You haven't answered the question," Trex yelled at the communo.

"We don't know," Srik wailed. "Communications are disrupted. Reports are disjointed. A state of chaos prevails in the city."

"Is the lab protected?" Trex demanded.

"Certainly! At least on three sides."

"What about the fourth?" I asked. It seemed like a reasonable question.

"We don't know," Srik wailed. "Communications have been totally disrupted. It is why I feared for you."

Trex and I exchanged glances. Stopping a handful of security guys was one thing, taking on a couple of hundred or more was something else—namely a losing proposition.

The director didn't have to be told; he was up on his feet in a flash, heading for the west wall computer.

"Hello, hello," Srik called, the note of hysteria back in his voice. "Director Trex, is everything all right?"

"Uh uh," I said, "but he's working on it—I think." I clicked off the communo, planted myself on the director's desk, and took a look-see.

Trex had reached the computer, was frantically pulling down on a long lever. He stepped back, stared up at the dome. I followed his gaze. The dome had begun to glow a milky white. It wasn't much of an improvement decoratively, but no doubt, it had another purpose. I sure hoped so, at least.

A thin smile crossed the director's face.

"Must be something good," Laura said, "or he wouldn't be smiling."

"Probably gone insane," I told her. "They often smile when they go insane."

Trex rejoined us, stood taking in his domain. "I have activated the seal," he said.

"Is that like 'certified and government approved'?" Laura asked.

"I certainly approve of it," Trex said smugly, "since I *am* the government. You've done well, Dunjer. My army will handle the rest of them out there, have no fear."

"Actually, I wasn't sweating it," I told him.

"We don't really live here, you know," Laura said.

"Yeah," I said, "we can always go home."

"So you can," Trex said, a bit sourly.

"But we wish you well," I said.

"Yes," Laura said, "you're a right-on guy for a dictator."

"Doubtless," Trex said.

"So, what's this seal, already?" Laura asked.

Trex allowed himself a broad, satisfied smile. "It is

a function of the Destabilizer, a small by-product, you might say.''

"Yeah, I might," I said, "if I knew what you were talking about."

"As long as that lever remains down," Trex said, "we are sealed in."

"In," I said. "As in 'can't get out'?"

"Precisely."

"We can get out," I assured him.

"Not through the dome."

"There're other ways."

"Ah, you mean Sass' device?"

"That's what I mean," I said.

"Quite right. You could go back to your dimension. But the enemy is sealed out of the dome."

"As in 'can't get in,' " Laura said.

"Well put," the director said.

"She's got a way with words," I said.

"It is my first test of this aspect of the Destabilizer," Trex said. "A minor aspect, to be sure, but one, as you see, that does have its uses."

"You sure it's working okay?" I asked.

He nodded toward the computer. "That vector tells me so."

"Glad you're on speaking terms. Mind if I put a mech on guard duty?"

Trex didn't. I beeped my instructions and a mech ambled over to stand watch.

"Where do we put the prisoners?" I asked.

"Leave them here. When the army has suppressed the revolt, they will be removed to more suitable quarters."

"The stockade, eh, to await court-martial?"

"Prison, to await execution. The time for pleasantries is long past, Mr. Dunjer."

I nodded, my collar starting to feel a bit tight. "Well, this time the job really *is* done," I said. "Guver's the guy you want, Trex, and your boys can round him up a lot easier than my mechs. So unless there's some special reason for us to stick around, we'll collect our fee and be on our way."

"Five gold bars for two days' service, I believe?"

"Your belief is well founded."

"I will make it seven."

"Very generous," I said. "A bonus for a job well done."

"A bonus for remaining a short while longer."

"What's a short while?"

"Until the Third Mobile Battalion arrives and takes charge of the city."

"Sort of keep our mech at the lever," Laura said.

"And everywhere else," Trex said. "I need you to maintain security in this complex. Guver has an entire floor here. Have you searched it?"

"Sure."

"Personally?"

"Grow up, Trex. We've got spy cubes planted there. My chief mech would've raised a holler if someone were still prowling around."

"You are certain?"

I beeped my beeper. "Anything cooking on the security floor?" I asked XX41.

"It's empty, skipper."

I beeped off. "Yeah, I'm certain."

"And the rest of the building?" Trex demanded.

"Ditto," I said.

"And you guarantee it will remain that way?"

"Talk sense, Trex."

"My staff are laymen when it comes to these matters. It is imperative, Mr. Dunjer, that you remain. It seems a reasonable request."

"An eighth bar would make it even more reasonable," I pointed out.

"Done."

"You're a hard man, Trex," I said, "but fair. You'll want to hustle up the bars now, and give 'em to one of my mechs for safekeeping."

"I will?"

"Sure. Just in case this seal of yours springs a leak and my team has to take off fast."

"You would desert me in my hour of need?"

"Director Trex," Laura said, "we didn't hire on as mercenaries."

"Wars are your baby," I told him, "security ours. We'll mosey along now and check out your building. If you need us, just whistle."

"Whistle?"

"Tell one of the mechs; it's the same thing."

"Gold bars, yet," Laura said.

"You expect me to take his check?"

"I was kind of hoping for something else."

"A free pass to the local entertainies?"

"More along the lines of a chest full of jewels, kiddo."

"Your chest doesn't need any jewels, sweetie," I told her. "It looks fine the way it is."

"Thanks, chief."

"The remark was personal, not professional. And with the bonus you'll pull down for this gig, you'll be able to buy a choice bauble back in Happy City."

"They come out of Cracker Jack boxes in Happy City."

"Yeah, but they're homegrown. It's the patriotic way."

"Aren't you two at all interested in what's happening on the monitor?" XX41 said.

"Why? Something's happening?" I asked.

"No, but it could be."

" 'Let a strong metal hand do your chores for you,' " I reminded it.

"That's just our cover."

"Hell, you had me fooled," I said.

We were seated in the laundry room, out of harm's way, at least for the moment. The door was closed and no sounds of combat penetrated into our hideaway. I stole a glance at the monitor. We had spy cubes planted out in the city, in the security ministry, and throughout the science complex. The monitor was casually flipping from one to the other. Outside, lots of people were busy shooting one another, standard procedure in this type of fracas. No big guns had been brought into play yet. Buildings were still intact. Neither side, apparently, wanted to louse up property values. Who could blame 'em? Both army and security forces called this neck of the woods home, probably brought their euphorics from the same euphor shop. I wondered if the UI would be as thoughtful if they ever got going. I hoped I wouldn't be around to find out.

No one seemed to be home at the Security Ministry. Probably out on the streets joining in the fun.

The monitor switched to the science complex. Not every floor and stairwell was staked out with a spy cube, but the ones that were didn't show me anything I didn't know. Just as well; I wasn't up to any big surprises.

"Spot anything?" I asked Laura.

"Nothing."

"Me either."

"We go back to small talk?" she said.

"Anything's better than watching that monitor."

I rose to my feet, fished in a pocket, pulled out a monitor cube and thumbed it to Fields.

"Going to earn that last brick, I see," Laura said.

"Just checking Trex's seal," I said, squinting at the cube.

"And? We still safe?"

"Hmmmm," I said sagely.

"That mean yes, no, or maybe?"

"It means," I said, "the cube registers two fields."

"Two?"

"Yeah. One around the dome, and one cutting right through it."

"I thought nothing could penetrate his seal."

"Maybe that's his seal too. Seems to be coming from below us somewhere."

"So what are we going to do?"

"Ask him."

"Nuts. That's how we always get in trouble."

CHAPTER **13**

"**I**mpossible," Trex said, looking annoyed.

Laura and I were back in his lab. Except for the prisoners and mechs over in one corner, everyone seemed to be carrying on as usual. Scientific detachment. Or maybe this whole crew had gone around the bend. If anything, their pace had become even more frantic.

"The cube doesn't lie," I said.

The director scowled at it impatiently as if I were showing him porno slides in the middle of his workday. "The seal is impermeable, Mr. Dunjer. Both to other fields and to all objects. That is its function. And according to my monitors, it is functioning perfectly. More then can be said for some others at the moment."

"Then how do you explain this?" I said, waving the cube at him. A guy with eight gold bars coming can afford to take an occasional dumb insult in stride. I hoped I was big enough to be that guy.

"I don't have to explain it, Mr. Dunjer. But if you press me I would say malfunction. Provided your idiotic cube functions at all. Your job is to maintain security here, not meddle in scientific matters beyond your understanding. Now you must really excuse me. We are at a critical juncture in our work. Absolutely critical. The Ul are restive. We must be prepared for the very worst."

He turned on his heel and hurried back to his desk. Laura and I stood staring after him. There was no profit in it.

"Even in another dimension," I complained, "we get hired by crackpots."

"What's the worst?" Laura asked.

"For him, that some other crackpot gets to call the tune. For us, that we don't get paid." I beeped X17, over by the wall. "Someone turn up with our fee yet?"

"If you mean the box with the eight gold bars," the mech said, "X3 has it. Although I must say, this soft metal is hardly functional."

"Either are you in clammy weather." To Laura I said, "The worst hasn't happened."

"Maybe not *this* worst, kiddo. But we're all up for grabs as long as we hang around here."

I beeped XX41. "Any sign of the Third Battalion in the city?"

"Not yet, boss."

"Keep me posted." I beeped off.

"So what's our next move?" Laura said. "Or don't we have one?"

"Sure we have one. Remember our motto: Never leave a bar unturned."

"That's *stone*."

"So it is, sweetie. What we do—as long as we're still stuck here—is hunt down this other field."

"*That's* what we do?"

"Listen, I don't like this cracker casting dispersions on our Security Plus product. Next thing you know, he'll want his eighth bar back."

"You have no faith in humanity, do you?"

"We're in another dimension, honey. What makes you think this guy's got anything to do with humanity?"

"We should have gotten a map," Laura said.

"Shhhh," I said eyeing the cube. "High-powered tech has made maps obsolete. Us too, probably. We keep going left here."

"Where's here?"

"You've got a point," I admitted.

We'd taken the lift down to ground level. A wide staircase got us to the basement in style. A narrower, less appetizing set of stairs—full of dust and an occasional cobweb—led to a dark subbasement. The cube pointed left, past a bunch of crates, cleaning equipment, pieces of dismantled machinery, and some other junk I couldn't identify. Our trek ended at a blank wall. Something I should have been used to by now, considering the business I was in.

"Maybe the cube *is* on the blink, Thomas."

"Our products last a lifetime," I said. "I wrote the brochure myself."

I felt around the wall, peered up at the ceiling, got down on hands and knees and poked around. Aside from plenty of dust I didn't find anything.

"So?" she said.

I climbed to my feet. "This is tricky."

"Not tricky—silly. You heard Trex: this isn't our job, let alone our world. Time to call it quits. Go guard our gold, entertain our mechs, do something important like pester the scientists. Anything but *this*."

"A sec, sweetie." I dug another cube out of my pocket, aimed it at the door. "I don't lug around all this hardware for kicks."

"Dementia has set in," she said. "You figure you're back in Happy City?"

The cube was a master key for all Security Plus locks. It also opened other locks back home, built along the same lines. Great for safecraking, illegal entry, and getting into high-priced theatres through the back door. Of course, we weren't back home; that could prove a hindrance.

"This world isn't so advanced," I said, thumbing the cube. "In fact, in lots of ways, it's downright primitive."

As if taking my words to heart, the wall obediently rumbled up into the ceiling. Laura and I stood staring at the dark, musty-smelling opening. I was a bit surprised myself.

"Now you've done it, kiddo," she said, "come up with a challenge your primitive mind won't be able to resist."

"Magalone's primitive—*we're* advanced. Try to get that straight, eh?"

I fished out my miniflash, sent a long beam through the uninviting doorway. A rusty ladder led down into total darkness. The dumb cube could sure pick 'em.

"It's creepy, Thomas. Let's not go in."

I stood tall, or as tall as a guy weighted down by cubes

can get. "This whole world's creepy. *I've* been called creepy."

"You *are* creepy."

"But that's never stopped a Security Plus op."

"That's because they're mostly mechs."

"C'mon."

"You're just one big nutty kid, aren't you?"

"Maybe. But the old cubes aren't the only Happy City products I've got handy."

"Yes, you've got me, and I don't want to go."

"Ah, you forget the peerless Happy City laser."

"Thanks, I've got my own."

"That makes two. And the nonpareil Happy City beeper. Watch." I beeped the beeper. "Get a couple of mechs to fix on my monitor cube and join us on the double."

"You up to some mischief, skipper?" XX41 asked.

"No more than usual. But maybe someone else is." I beeped off.

We started down.

Our footsteps echoed over the cracked, pitted concrete. My miniflash cut a wide slice through the darkness. The place had all the charm and beguiling odor of a disused sewer. Since we were in an old, abandoned sewer tunnel under the lab, that made sense. The monitor pointed us in the direction of the vertical field. We followed.

"Is this worth the effort?" Laura said.

"Probably not. But every now and then I like to show the mechs we can handle things on our own."

"You sent for backup."

"Not that much on our own."

We rounded a bend. More empty tunnel stretched before us. We slowed to a reasonable trot. Maybe the first reasonable thing I'd done in a while.

The beeper beeped. "You've got company, chief."

"Eh?"

"I've a radar fix on you, boss," XX41 said. "The monitor shows a clump of figures off to your right."

"How many is a clump?"

"Can't tell; they're bunched together."

"They moving toward us?"

"Parallel. They're in another tunnel."

I consulted the cube. Parallel seemed to be in the direction of the second field. "Seemed" was the operative word. Though it wasn't too likely that someone was strolling around here just now for his health.

"Any way to reach 'em?"

"There's a passage up ahead that connects your tunnel to theirs. If you hurry you might be able to intercept them."

"Thanks, XX41."

"And have no fear, skipper, if you get into hot water, the mechs will rescue you. They're right on your heels. Almost."

"I can hardly wait." I beeped off.

"Shouldn't we hang around for them, Thomas?"

"And miss the fun?" I broke into a trot, Laura behind me.

"Some fun."

"Look," I said, "this clump—whoever they are—doesn't have fancy radar to warn 'em like we do. We can sneak up, get an eyeful before they know what hit 'em."

"Hitting, yet. And this isn't even our war."

The passage, when we came to it, was nothing to brag

about. It was low, narrow, and seemed best suited for canine travel. Just looking at it made me feel claustrophobic. If it wasn't for the presence of Laura, I'd've probably given the whole enterprise plenty of second thought. Or at least waited for the mechs. Now I'd have to be a hero.

"After you, kid," I said.

"Thomas!"

"Just kidding."

I glanced behind me, shone my flash around. No sign of the mechs. Maybe they'd stopped for a red light? Stooping over, I headed into the passage. My shoulders scraped against both walls, part of my back touched the ceiling. My light showed only darkness ahead. I inched my way forward, wondering if the place was infested with rats or other unpleasant life-forms.

"I think I'll stick to the office from now on," Laura said behind me.

"That'll make two of us."

It took a while before we neared the end of the passage. I doused the light, shuffled a last few feet, stuck my head out. I saw and heard nothing. Stepping out, I straightened, held out a hand to Laura.

"So where's this devious clump we're pursuing?" she whispered when she was by my side.

"Probably done the smart thing and gone back." I beeped XX41. "We alone down here?"

"You were too slow, skipper, you missed them. Do your joints need oiling?"

"No, but the mechs you sent along probably do. Where are they?"

"Right behind you, boss," a voice said. "X6 and X7 reporting for duty."

I turned to Laura. "I must be okay, I usually faint when they do that." To the beeper I said, "Our quarry change direction?"

"No. They're about five minutes ahead of you and moving fast."

I nodded at the mechs. "All right, guys, go sic 'em."

CHAPTER **14**

The pair of mechs didn't wait for more idle chitchat. They took off down the tunnel as if running the Happy City marathon. In a moment they'd vanished in the darkness. I shone my flash over the ground, up the walls. This place was bigger than the old sewer, if not any more delightful. Rails ran across the ground.

"Could've taken a trolley down here," I said, "if we'd only known."

"It would have been a long wait."

"Yeah, let's hoof it."

Laura and I followed the mechs, but with a lot less energy then they'd displayed. Maybe our batteries had run down. By the time we reached them they'd have corralled and hog-tied the clump, claiming all the honor but saving us human ops a lot of wear and tear. It seemed an all right bargain.

A large *boom* sounded from up ahead.

"Jeez," I said.

My beeper beeped at once. "Boss," X7 said, "there's a problem."

"Brought in the big guns, eh?"

"Prescient as always, boss."

"Also," Laura said, "his hearing's not too bad."

"You taken cover?" I said.

"Boss, what a question. We wouldn't be talking to you now if we hadn't."

"Don't do anything rash," I said.

"Heaven forbid!"

"I'm on my way."

"A few more mechanicals wouldn't hurt either," X6 chimed in. "*You're* even more fragile than we are."

I beeped off. "They've been hanging around with XX41 too long," I said. I beeped the culprit. "A couple more mechs down here. We've run into trouble."

"Will do, skipper. But I've a report there's trouble up here too. The scientists are in a tizzy."

"Any special reason?"

"They won't say. I think they lack a fundamental respect for the noble mechanical."

"Keep our boys asking. The clump still moving?"

"The clump has separated into three distinct figures, chief. One has merged with an outcrop of some kind. A long object is protruding from it, which could very well be a weapon. The other pair are engaged in stationary activity of some kind."

"Can we get behind 'em?"

"There are passageways," XX41 said, "from one tunnel to the other all the way up the line."

"Beep me when we get to the right one." I beeped off.

Laura said, "We crawl back to the sewer, huh?"

"Yeah, unless you want to go and see what's biting the director."

"I'd rather face the guns."

"Who wouldn't?"

I turned and ducked back into the passage.

"Remember one thing, Thomas," Laura said behind me. "We *are* fragile."

"Don't worry, I've been hanging out with XX41, too."

I lay in darkness—Laura by my side—flat on the ground. There's something about crawling along an old tunnel on your belly, and that something is lousy. Coming to a halt hadn't improved matters much.

Up ahead, a lone lamp brought light to the scene. In its glare I saw an ancient, battered, rust covered rail cart. Behind it, his back to us, a man crouched; his hands weren't empty. The nozzle of a projectile weapon stuck out over the cart like a flagpole laying claim to a patch of turf.

Between the cart and us two guys were very busy, engaged in what XX41's radar had seen as stationary activity. It wasn't all that stationary. They were digging, flailing away at the ground with a rusty pick and shovel that looked as if it'd come straight out of the rail cart. The guy by the cart and one of the diggers wore the black uniforms of the security forces. The third lad was Guver.

"Pay dirt," I whispered.

"Practicing for prison," Laura said. "All they need is the ball and chain."

"Looks like a makeshift operation," I whispered. "These boys have automat implements for this kind of work. They didn't know they'd be digging."

"Better get the cube out."

"Right."

Thumbing the monitor cube back on Fields, I took a gander, held it out to Laura. "The end of the rainbow," she said.

"Whatever *that* is." The second field shot out of the ground directly at Guver's feet.

"Must be important," she said, "for them to be doing this now."

"I almost hate to interrupt 'em," I said. I beeped X6 and his pal. "Lob some firepower at the cart, and come running."

"Aye, aye, chief."

"Try not to overshoot, guys, or you'll get *us*."

"And face unemployment? You know us better than that, boss."

The pair didn't wait on ceremony. The cart seemed to jump in the air as if showing off a new skill that might yet get it out of the tunnel. The shooter was thrown back, wrestling to hold on to his gun. Guver and his cohort whirled toward the commotion.

My laser was out. I was up on my feet and running.

"Drop it!" I bawled at the shooter in my best crime-stopper manner. It had the usual effect: he ignored me.

The guy started to swing his gun my way. I was ready. I aimed a laser blast at the nozzle, cut loose. The nozzle melted over like ice cream in a broiler.

Guver's buddy had his pistol out, a fast man on the

draw. Too fast for his own good. Laura shot him. He made an unpleasant gurgling sound and fell over backward.

"Don't move!" my pair of mechs yelled in unison as they came bounding out of the darkness.

No one even thought of moving anymore. The shooter had dropped his gun, raised his hands, was standing stock-still in an admirable attempt to avoid his chum's fate.

Guver was frozen like a chunk of ice in a midwinter snowstorm—his mouth open, his eyes bulging, his hand halfway to his holster. The guy looked like he was having a fit. "You fool!" he screamed at me. I didn't take it to heart. The security chief had never been much of a fan of mine.

"Hey, can't win 'em all," I said sagely. "Don't be a sore loser, pal."

"We'll all die!" he screamed.

"Sure," I agreed, "some of us sooner than later. You right away, if you don't shut up."

"Anyone send for us?" two new voices called out in unison. X11 and X19 had joined us.

"Sorry, fireworks are over, guys."

"We can live with it," they chorused.

"Yeah, live. Disarm this guy," I said, nodding toward Guver, "frisk the other pair, see if there's anything you can do for the one on the ground."

"You must dig up the beacon!" Guver shrieked. "At once!"

"He's still giving orders," Laura said.

"Reflex action, probably."

"I could shoot him," she said.

"Let Trex do it; he enjoys that stuff."

"This one," X11 said, bending over the fallen trooper, "needs medical attention."

"Run him up to the clinic," I said.

"To hear is to obey, oh, boss of bosses." X11 stooped down, gently picked up the trooper, and took off.

"Beats waiting around for an ambulance, eh?"

"Sure does, oh, boss of bosses," Laura said.

"Don't you understand," Guver shouted, "we'll all die *now* if you don't dig up that beacon and destroy it!"

He had my attention. "How's that?" I wanted to know.

The security chief had broken into a sweat. "The beacon belongs to the Ul."

"They want it back?" I said.

Guver had started to shake. "It is buried here. It is a homing device. It will guide the Ul energy weapons."

"You doubt Trex's seal?"

"This device renders the seal useless. It will not hold in the face of an all-out attack."

"So who says they're going to attack?" Laura asked. "Even if what you say is remotely true."

"Excuse me," X7 said, "there does appear to be some sort of energy buildup on the seal."

"Not that we were eavesdropping," X6 said, "but the scientists sounded quite alarmed."

"Quite. However," X7 said, "the buildup is still deemed insignificant by those in the know."

I said, "You got this while guarding the prisoners?"

"Being thought of as an inanimate object," X6 said, "has its occasional uses. The seal, so far, is said to be holding fast, boss."

"You know anything about this?" I asked X19.

"They speak truth. When I left, the situation was unchanged."

"There may still be time," Guver said, wiping his brow with a shaky hand. "Listen, the Ul employ many spies. The entire city is honeycombed with their cells, no one cell knowing what the other is up to."

"But as security chief," I said, "you had an inkling."

"Of course. I knew about Litsh's cell, had them all under surveillance. But only when you brought them in did I fully see the extent of their duplicity."

"You can't trust some people," I agreed.

"This man Litsh," he said, "even outranks *me*."

"Good janitors are hard to find," I said.

"The two technicians, Argick and Bluch, gave him the secrets of the Destabilizer."

"Trex didn't seem too worried," I said. "And if he isn't, why should we be?"

Guver scowled. "He underestimates the Ul, just as he does everyone else. Don't you see?"

"Not really," I said.

"From what Litsh and other cells gave them—from what I gave them myself!—the Ul pieced together enough of the Destabilizer to devise a weapon against it."

"This beacon, eh?"

He nodded. "The beacon was placed here long ago."

"But not by you, pal?"

"By parties from one of the Ul cells. The task was to adjust it by remote control to match the frequency of the seal. For that the properties of the seal had to be known. It is this riddle the Ul have succeeded in unraveling."

I said, "You didn't know this thing was buried here?"

"The Ul told me of its existence," he said, "but not its whereabouts."

"An understandable lack of trust," I said. "Even for the trusting Ul."

"Especially if they got to know him," Laura said.

"When the seal was activated," Guver said, "our security monitors picked up the beacon too."

"Right in the middle of your coup," I pointed out.

"I tried to head off the attack!"

"You're a damn patriot," I said.

"I had no choice. The Ul never responded to Litsh's last broadcast, the one you interrupted. It meant they no longer needed the data he was supplying—they were ready to make their move. I saw my duty then, to hand over the city to the Ul before they attacked."

"Some duty," Laura said.

"The alternative was total destruction!"

"And then your coup flopped," I said.

"We'd have won the day if your miserable metal men hadn't held the lab."

"I think that's a compliment," X6 said.

"Don't bank on it," Laura said.

"When we knocked the props out from under you," I said, "you went hunting for the beacon."

"We too have our high-tech devices. Yes, I followed it here. And once more you have seen fit to interfere."

"It's the nature of his calling," Laura said.

"I get these urges," I said.

"If Magalone is destroyed, it will be your fault, Dunjer."

"Put it in writing," I said, "so I can collect from the Ul."

Guver stamped his foot. "Every minute counts! Why are you not digging up the homing beacon?"

"Yes, boss, why not?" X19 asked.

"Because," Laura said, "he has great faith in Trex's judgment."

"Hmmmm," I said.

I got out the monitor cube, took a look-see. I shook my head. "Your pick and shovel, Guver, wouldn't've got you very far. This device is way down there."

"I could blast it," X19 said.

"We all could," the other two mechs chimed in.

"Why not?" I said. "Let's humor this guy."

The human contingent stepped far back. I kept my laser on Guver and his pal, nodded at the mechs, who had cautiously retreated, too. Each extended an arm. The hand part smartly flipped up and back, revealing a nice-sized barrel that doubled as a forearm.

They cut loose at the ground. There was plenty of noise, flame, and flying dirt.

When the smoke cleared I ambled over, looked down. "Big hole," I said. I took a gander at the cube. "Good work, guys."

"It's gone?" Laura said.

"Gone," I said, "as though it never existed." I grinned at our prisoner. "Satisfied, pal?"

Guver let out his breath.

And the ground began to shake and rumble as if enraged that we'd dared blast it.

"What the hell's that?" I said.

As if in answer, from far off, a siren began to shriek.

CHAPTER 15

In the wavering light, Guver turned parchment white. "Magalone is under siege," he croaked. "You're too late, Dunjer."

"Couldn't be a fire drill, I suppose," Laura said.

"We'll know soon enough." I beeped XX41. "What's cooking?"

"Maybe us, skipper."

"You don't know?"

"I was going to beep you when I did. Trex isn't talking, but I think his seal is going down."

"We under attack?"

"If not now, any minute maybe."

"Security forces aren't storming the lab, are they?"

"Not so you'd notice, chief. The fighting's stopped in the city. Everyone's run for cover."

"There is no cover from the Ul," Guver moaned. "We are all doomed."

"The Ul, eh?"

"Either them," the mech said, "or some enemy they neglected to mention."

"Stand by," I said. "We may have to pull up stakes fast."

"I wasn't going anywhere."

I beeped off. "This tunnel have a quick way out?" I asked X19.

"Quick enough," it said. "I got here in no time flat."

"That's the right speed for beating it," I said.

Laura said, "We jog it?"

"We go in style, sweetie—piggyback."

"Some style."

I nodded at the trooper. "You're on your own, pal."

The guy looked around wildly as if hunting for some safe place to hide from an Ul assault. He didn't bother saying bye-bye. He turned tail and dashed up the tunnel.

"Okay, Guver, alley-oop."

"Alley-oop?" he said weakly, as though another calamity was in the making.

"Yeah, like this."

The mechs had sunk to one knee as if about to propose to some stunning metal lady. Laura and I hopped on their backs. Years of training had somehow failed to make this mode of transport any less embarrassing. Guver hesitated for an instant as though reluctant to expose himself to this last indignity before certain demise. Then he followed our example. No one wants to kick the bucket alone in a dark tunnel, not even a security chief.

We got out of there in triple time.

* * *

The lab looked like the local loony bin after the inmates had been let loose to run the joint. Techs and scientists were careening into one another as they sprinted from one end of the lab to the other, like misplaced basketball players, turning dials, pushing levers, punching keyboards. I hoped more than panic was at work here. At least they hadn't powdered out—probably because there was no place to go.

Another change had occurred in my absence. The dome was now a milky pink, punctuated by flashes of bright red. I didn't think the change was meant to be an improvement.

Not less than half an hour ago, Guver was the most wanted guy in town. Now, no one gave him—or us—a second glance.

The great man himself, Trex, was at his desk, glowering at a monitor and punching keys frantically. He seemed oblivious of his surroundings.

"I don't think they need us anymore," Laura said.

"Probably never did in the first place," I said. "Nailing Guver here still leaves the Ul, and they're a problem we can't handle."

"I tried to contact them," Guver whispered hoarsely, "I tried. They wouldn't respond. They are sacrificing us all, their whole network . . ."

"Those are the breaks, pal. You should've picked nicer guys to sell out to." I beeped XX41. "Anything doing in the city?"

"Only a large-scale riot, skipper. Everyone's trying to leave town, but the dome has only a few exits."

"Okay. Call in any stray mechs and get up here on the double."

I beeped off, told X19 to keep an eye on Guver, took

my sidekick by the arm, and started out for the director. It felt like crossing Happy City's main drag—the one known as Death's Juncture—against the red light.

The dome, I noticed, was showing more red than pink now, a sight that didn't warm my heart.

"Trex!" I bawled when I was standing over his desk. Even that barely got his attention. His eyes flickered in my direction for the briefest moment.

"Go away, Mr. Dunjer," he muttered.

"What's happening, Trex? You owe us that much!"

"I owe you nothing—you have your gold." His eyes returned to the monitor, his fingers to the keyboard. "Do what you wish."

"Trex!" I yelled, "if you hadn't been so pigheaded, I'd've reached the Ul beacon sooner, and you and this whole bunch'd be sitting pretty now."

Again, the hazel eyes peered into mine. "The seal is still functioning, Mr. Dunjer. But they have taken its measure."

"It won't hold?"

"It can't. Its frequency was breached."

"So what's the next move?"

The director was back at his work. His lips twitched. "My last card."

"Eh?"

"Go now. This is our world, not yours."

Laura tugged at my arm. "I was just going to say that, Thomas, honest."

"My very words exactly," XX41 said over my shoulder. "Reporting for end of duty, sir."

"Everyone here?"

"All present and accounted for."

"That wraps it up, I guess." I stepped back from the

desk, reached into my pocket for Sass' cube, activated it. I let out a sigh. "That's it. The little guy'll be popping up any minute to whisk us away from here."

"Not a moment too soon, boss," the mech said.

"Yeah, but I hate to leave like this before the last act's played out."

"Why's that, skipper?"

"Because he's got a screw loose," Laura said.

"That often happens to mechs too," XX41 said.

"Sure," she said. "*You* we can fix."

"Come on, gang," I said, "enough small talk. We'll get run over here."

We began moving toward the east wall, bumping into shoulders, arms, stomachs. The hubbub was something to hear, had risen to fever pitch. People were screaming at each other, snapping out orders.

"What do you think they're going to do?" Laura asked.

I shrugged. "Mass prayer, maybe." I caught X19's eye. "Turn him loose," I yelled.

"Our number-one prisoner?" Laura complained.

"You want to take him back to Happy City?" I said. "He'd make a lousy trophy."

We stood, our backs to the wall, surveying the mayhem. It was not an inspiring sight. I glanced at Sass' cube. A small green light peered back at me stolidly. The cube was functioning, at least on this end. Now all Sass had to do was hold up his end of the bargain.

The tumult—as if joining me in contemplating this salient, and maybe regrettable fact—suddenly took a nosedive, sank near to the vanishing point.

I looked up with a start.

A lot of backs were to me, heads turned toward the director.

He was up on his feet, standing ramrod straight, as if being reviewed by the president. Only here, there was no president, just a director. And he was it. His eyes were fixed on an empty patch of floor that had just seconds ago been crammed full of people. Everyone was either eyeballing him or the empty space, even the prisoners and our contingent of mechs.

"I miss something?" I asked Laura.

"You weren't the only one," she said. "They must be using sneaky hand signals or something."

"He punched his keyboard," XX41 said, "and leaped to his feet. Is that significant?"

"You're asking me?"

There was still no sign of Sass. I glanced at his cube again; nothing had changed.

"Boss," XX41 said.

I looked up.

The empty space was slowly sliding back, becoming a huge hole. Something began to rise silently from under the floor, something that vaguely resembled a tapered, long-nosed, cannon.

"Jeez," I said. It didn't take a genius to figure the next move. The old boy was going to try and blast his way out of this mess. Good luck.

I felt Laura gripping my right arm, XX41, the left.

"We really don't want to be here, boss," the mech said. The understatement of the decade.

"Where's your buddy?" Laura asked urgently.

"Any second now," I said, my own voice sounding a bit squeaky in my ears. I was starting to break into a nice cold sweat.

Trex came out from behind his desk, grimly strode toward the gun.

The contraption was mounted on a pedestal. Five steps led up to a seat in front of a small monitor with a single row of keys beneath it.

Trex climbed the steps, seated himself. He didn't wave or make some final speech to the crowd. His hand reached out, touched a key. The four walls that were the lab computer instantly came to life. Multicolored lights began blinking on and off. Vectors, dials, gauges spun wildly. A series of symbols began to flash helter-skelter across a dozen screens. Under any other circumstances I might've enjoyed the show.

"What's happening?" I shouted at a fat tech in a white lab jacket. He ignored me.

The gun on the pedestal began to tilt upward toward the dome. The dome, I saw, was glowing an ominous bright red. But then, everything around here was ominous just now.

I felt my back trying to merge with the wall. Laura and XX41 had the same idea.

I stuck a clammy hand in my pocket, rummaged around among my now useless cubes, came up with Trex's gold coin, the one that blocked communication with the Knowledge Crystal.

"Hang on to this," I told Laura, dropping it in her palm.

"It brings good luck?"

"I'll let you know."

I made my mind a blank, or as blank as I could under the circumstances. Crystal! I thought. I peered at the mountain that was still poking its peak through the lab floor, got set to try again.

"Yes?" a voice went off in my noodle.

"Quick. Is there someplace to hide?"

"I'm afraid not. For either of us."

"No luck," I told Laura. To the Crystal I said, "Explain what's happening."

"I'd have done so earlier, you know, if you hadn't pocketed that silly coin. The director," it said, "is testing the Destabilizer."

"Testing?"

"Yes, it has never been used before, so this must be termed a test, mustn't it?"

"That's all, just a test?"

"Hardly all. He is also hoping to defend Magalone. He will use the weapon to that end."

"Great. Is it going to work?"

"How should I know?"

"It's some kind of cannon?"

"Only in appearance. It doesn't shoot shells, you know."

"So what does it shoot?"

"Nothing."

"Give me that again."

"The Destabilizer releases a wide field," the Crystal said, "that reduces objects to their atomic component."

"Makes mincemeat of 'em, eh?"

"No, atoms. In short, it destabilizes things."

"It's going to destabilize the red field on the seal?"

"Dear me, no. The seal is a goner."

"A goner?"

"Along with us," the Crystal said, "if Trex cannot stop the attack that will come raining down on us once the seal has totally disintegrated."

"So that's his game," I said.

"Believe me, it is no game."

I believed it. I wiped sweat from my brow, said, "You wouldn't know what happened to Dr. Sass, would you?"

"Certainly."

"Eh?" The dumb Crystal was full of surprises—so far all of them bad.

"He is outside the dome, between dimensions."

"What's he doing *there*?"

"Trying to get in, of course."

"Trying?"

"Alas, he cannot possibly succeed."

"Why the hell not?"

"He appeared, you see, a fraction of a second too late."

"I don't see."

"Once the Destabilizer was activated, your friend had no hope of entry. Its field acts as an impenetrable wall."

I thought fast. "What if the gizmo's turned off?"

"Why then, he could get in. But so could the UI's energy weapons."

"Only if the seal's down."

"True."

"It's not down now, is it?"

"Almost."

"We'll have to chance it."

"The director will never allow that."

"He won't have anything to say about it. How do you turn that damn thing off?"

"Simply press the large green button at the end of the keyboard."

"Thanks."

I used my beeper, beeped an all-mech alert. "At the word 'go,' rush Trex—the first one to reach him jabs the green button on his keyboard. *Go!*"

I had my laser out, was starting to move too, when I heard the loud popping sound. I looked up. The seal was gone.

"Too late," the Crystal said.

Trex pulled back on a lever.

White light filled the lab.

And exploded.

CHAPTER 16

It was dark.

The darkness was everywhere, spotted with bright swirling pinpoints of light that could've been stars.

That figured. Almost.

When you get bopped on the bean, you're supposed to see stars, and I was seeing plenty. The whole shebang seemed to stretch endlessly—right through the solar system and galaxy, out into the universe, and across some other kind of space, too. And I was stretching with it.

I wondered how I was pulling it off.

Especially with no body.

I was dead sure about the last item. For all I knew, I was dead and this was the Great Beyond. Only I didn't think so. I wasn't sure what I *did* think.

It didn't seem to matter.

The pinpoints of light kept twinkling, changing. As if the show were being put on for my benefit alone. I liked that. The whole thing was a hoot. Who needs a body, anyway?

I kept drifting farther out. Becoming more scattered, more attenuated. It didn't seem to make much difference.

And after a while, I heard the voices.

Voices were about right for this pickle; I wasn't a bit surprised to hear 'em—nothing could surprise me much anymore. They were coming in loud and clear, as though I'd cut into a party line on some rural phone system. They weren't real voices, and I heard no words. But I got their meaning, all right. It would've been tough to miss. Even for a guy with no ears.

They didn't come from anywhere I'd ever been before, which was just as well, because even on such short acquaintance, I didn't think I liked 'em a whole lot.

They had ambitions, were interested in a nice globe in this galaxy, one they could take over.

They were thinking big, something I could understand. Though the piece of real estate they wanted to latch onto, I gathered, wasn't all that big. Just your average, medium-sized world. They didn't seem to mind. And if they didn't, why should I? It was none of my business anyway.

I drifted on, expanding. Something these birds would've approved of: expansion was their game.

I was one with the universe, with time and space itself—we were buddies.

I knew what was happening. Knowing was one of my strong points out here—maybe my only one. I had no brain, but when had that ever stopped me? My consciousness was intact and going great guns. It seemed to embrace all reality. I knew that, but the details were kind of fuzzy. I didn't worry about it. I didn't worry about anything.

I wasn't sure how much time had gone by. Maybe only an instant, maybe a lot more. Time out here meant something else, was nothing I could measure.

Then I was reversing course.

Like a yo-yo, I felt myself beginning to reel in, to contract.

I must've gone beyond them, for the voices had faded out for a while. I hadn't noticed. Only now, suddenly, they were back, stronger then ever.

They sounded a bit peeved this time around. They were still working on their pet project, but it was now seen as merely a stepping-stone, a jumping-off point before they hit the rest of this galaxy. Oh, boy.

These babies weren't fooling. Their ambitions were growing by leaps and bounds: they wanted the whole pie. Or as much of the pie as they knew about. Only something was biting 'em, had gotten in the way of their real estate boom, and it had made 'em grouchy. I didn't hang around long enough to find out what it was.

They hadn't sounded all that nice before. They seemed downright mean spirited now. I was glad I was just passing through.

They were called the Klarr.

I kept shrinking.

The galaxy pulled me toward it, drew me in from the far corners of the universe.

The Klarr were gone.

I was moving faster now, rushing along like the Happy City locomotive on full throttle.

A thought struck me—I wondered why I'd been able

to hear these Klarr in the first place? No other sounds had registered on my trek.

Then the stars started to wink out.

And I was gone too.

CHAPTER 17

There was still a ball of darkness around me. Only this time it was icy cold.

I felt myself spinning like a speck of dust caught in a whirlpool. There was something neat about this darkness: it kind of lulled me. I wanted to crawl into its center, to drift off into nothingness. But the cold got to me instead, kept me from my rest. I flailed against it with arms and legs.

Like a huge balloon, I felt myself drifting upward. There was pain in my chest and a roaring in my ears. I flailed out some more; it seemed the smart thing to do—though mostly, smart and I had parted company. Vaguely, I noted my body was back. How about that?

The roar in my ears had turned into a very loud scream.

And my chest felt as if a sledgehammer were pounding on it.

I broke the water's surface, filled my burning lungs with air. I took a deep breath, then another. I looked around. I was still in darkness. Icy water splashed over my mouth, nose, and eyes. I choked, spit it out. A fog-horn sounded in the distance.

Time to do something decisive, show I was my own man. I opened my mouth, bawled into the darkness.

"Help!"

No answer came. So much for that.

A wave picked me up and dunked me under.

Great. I was running low on energy, coming unraveled like a windup toy. I wasn't going to hold my own much longer. Peering into the fog I thought I saw something that might've been a light off to the right.

Doubling over, I stuck my head back underwater, pulled off my shoes, surfaced, shoved them in my pocket with my cube collection, wiggled out of my jacket, and tied the sleeves around my neck.

I turned over on my side and began to swim.

I lay on the dock, more dead than alive, and gave what was left of my mind a workout. The last thing I remembered that made any sense at all was Trex unleashing his Destabilizer. I'd tried to stop him, and then the whole joint had gone blooey.

After that, it was all a mishmash.

I remembered floating through the cosmos, eaves-dropping on some nasty specimens called the Klarr. And then I was bobbing around in the drink.

The awful Klarr and my jaunt through the universe seemed like so much eyewash, a by-product of the lab blowup. But the rest of it was real enough.

So where was I?

Had I been blown clear out of the lab and into the Magalone bay? Uh uh. I wouldn't be lying around in one piece, in a puddle of water, trying to dope things out if I had. I'd've been atomized like a victim of Trex's dumb weapon.

Had Sass popped up at the last minute to carry us all to safety—only to get blasted off course by the explosion?

So where was he? Not to mention Laura and the rest of the gang?

And if none of those things had happened, what had?

I didn't have a clue.

I thought of getting up, snooping around a bit, seeing what's what. The usual good old high-tech sleuthing stuff. I didn't do it. What I did wasn't recommended in the Detective's Handbook. But sometimes a guy has to improvise.

I closed my eyes and went to sleep.

"Come on, mate."

Someone was shaking my shoulder. I tried to pull away, but the shaker had a talonlike grip. I groaned, opened my eyes.

A large, unshaven head swam into view above me. "Don't wanna be here when the Spiffies show up, mate."

"Eh?" I said, with my usual show of prebreakfast brilliance.

"The Spiffies, mate, they'll be here any minute."

I tried to move. My body felt as if I'd been snoozing on a slab of metal. But it had only been a wooden dock. Only. I was ready for a long stay in the nearest rehab center. Or retirement at full pay. I wondered if they had any of those nice things in this neck of the woods. I wondered where this neck of the woods was; it'd make a difference.

Bits and pieces of yesterday's doings flitted through my mind like stray wasps. I didn't bother making sense of 'em. I wasn't sure there was any.

I sat up slowly, reluctantly, as if my joints and muscles had rusted overnight.

"Hurry, mate, they're coming."

I didn't know what the Spiffies were. But I had a hunch I might not enjoy meeting 'em just now.

My jacket sleeves were still tied around my neck, not unlike a noose. I untied them, shrugged into the jacket. I dug my shoes out of a pocket, put them on over my self-cleaning socks.

The short, stocky guy held out a hand, helped me to my feet. My grime-repellent suit immediately recreased itself, resumed its customary spic-and-span appearance. The suit was in better shape than me.

My new pal gawked at it. "Damned if I ever saw anything like that, mate."

"Doesn't tear either," I said, always glad to boost a Happy City product.

He looked at me doubtfully. "You sure you're an Outie?"

I nodded. I certainly wasn't part of any in-group around here. And right now I needed a local who knew the ropes.

He cocked his head. "Come on, then. Standing around here will just get us both in trouble."

I followed him through a maze of back alleys in what looked like an industrial sector of some kind—mostly loft buildings and factories. Looks can fool you when you only see the back side of things, but the grime was a dead giveaway. I caught glimpses of smaller structures stuck between the large ones. I thought of asking what they were, only this didn't seem like the moment to spotlight my ignorance.

We didn't talk. From time to time I heard voices out on the street. They made my guide jumpy; he hustled even more. I knew fear when I saw it. A rotten notion began drifting through my noodle. Had I somehow crossed the line, landed in Ul territory? What I knew about the Ul added up to zero—except that for Trex they were the bad guys. I could've kicked myself, all right, but that was hardly proper treatment for a guy I admired so much.

Without my mechs to back my play, I was on my own. Just like the good old days. Only, the good old days hadn't been all that swell, had they?

The whole area looked like an army base. Or a kiddies' camp. There were single-story barracks everywhere. One of the barracks had two stories. Admin, my guide told me. We skirted it, worked our way through a bunch of gravel paths between the buildings, stopped at one that resembled all the others.

We went in the back way.

There were a few dozen aisles of cots stretching toward a far wall. A couple still held sleeping men, the rest were empty. About a half dozen guys were up and moving around. They kept looking my way, but none came over for a close-up gander. They were either well trained or very timid.

For a second I figured I'd been drafted or landed in some kind of prison—two prospects worth avoiding at all costs. The setting, though, seemed a mite informal for that.

"Come on, mate," my host said. "Let's chow up." And he rubbed his hands together eagerly.

The line crept forward. My pal and I were stuck way at the end. He wasn't much for small talk, which was just as well. I wasn't ready for it yet. Maybe I'd never be.

I glanced ahead.

The mushy brownish-yellowish stuff they were dishing out at the steam table might've been oatmeal, but probably wasn't. The hot green beverage sure as hell wasn't coffee. Some odor that smelled like disinfectant made my stomach cringe. I hoped it came from the floor and not the grub. My Security Plus Handy Food Tester was handy back in Happy City, not here where I needed it. Giving the job to me. Being poisoned, though, was better then starving to death. Poisoned, you still have a fighting chance. Sometimes.

For a guy with no local currency, the price at least was right. No one seemed to be paying for the gunk. Maybe I'd hit the local soup kitchen?

Sizing up the eaters, I saw what seemed to be lots of ordinary joes, working stiffs in coarse gray clothes. They looked a bit grim as if their union dues came to more than their weekly paychecks.

Some others looked like toughs, wore wide leather belts and calf-high boots. That meant nothing. What did was the way they held themselves. They were the type of guys you wouldn't want stomping on your face.

There were bums, their baggy clothes soiled and wrinkled, sticking to their own kind at tables over by the south wall. They ate quickly, bent low over their bowls, as if afraid someone might snatch 'em away.

The guys in line had their backs to us. But some at the tables had started giving me the eye. You couldn't blame 'em. My Happy City duds made me a standout, a real fashion plate in this crowd.

That gave me an idea.

I led the way after we got our chow, lugged my tray over to a corner workingman's table near the wall. I'd've liked one with a bit more privacy, but in this joint that was as likely as getting served a steak for breakfast.

All the tables were long, meant to seat some two dozen. I parked myself across from my pal, at the far end, my back to the north wall for that extrasecure feeling. The seven guys who shared our table gave us plenty of room.

My short pal dug into his glop. I took a taste of mine. It would never pass for real food, but it wasn't exactly loathsome. I polished it all off. The green liquid was no great shakes but I got that down too. When I didn't keel over from toxic food poisoning, I figured I might survive a while longer.

I said, "What's your name?"

"Ixil," he said.

I nodded. I'd found more reasonable names in Magalone, and theirs were plain screwy. "Dunjer's mine."

Ixil gave me a searching look. "Never heard a name like that before, mate."

"Not in these parts," I said.

He looked at me. And his gaze turned shifty. The notion that I was a stranger wasn't bringing much instant cheer into his life.

"You said you was an Outie."

I shrugged a shoulder.

Four seats up the table, a tall party had been cocking an ear in our direction. He abruptly got up and left.

I said, "What were you doing down at the dock?"

He licked his lips, glanced around as if to see if anyone else might want to answer the question. "I'm a scout, mate," he said.

"Uh huh," I said. "And what's that?"

"Everyone knows what a scout is."

"Tell me anyway."

"Pick up the strays."

"Strays," I said.

Ixil was sweating. "Want me to tell you that one too?"

"Uh huh."

"Outies that don't come in after curfew."

I smiled at him. "Against the law," I said quietly. I wasn't guessing. Trotting tight-lipped through the back alleys gave the game away.

He fidgeted. "Everyone knows there's scouts," he said. "An Outie steps outta line, has a snifter too many, his mates gotta look after him."

"The Spiffies know?"

He wagged his head.

"They wink at it, eh?"

"Sure."

"Unless," I said, "they catch you red-handed."

At the words "red-handed" another worker hurriedly rose and scampered off.

"This some kinda test?" Ixil asked hoarsely.

"Ixil," I said, "*I* ask the questions, *you* answer them. Got that?" By the power vested in my nonpareil Happy City suit, I thought, but shrewdly kept that part to myself.

"I ain't in trouble, am I?"

"You're fine," I told him, "as long as you give me the straight goods."

"What's that?"

"Why, the world as you see it, Ixil."

"The world?"

"We start small. In here. Who are these guys?"

Ixil glanced around as if curious himself. "Why, Outies, mate."

"Labor, muscle, bums."

He nodded vigorously as though I'd hit on some great universal truth. "They work the plants. Gotta work the plants, you know, keep them going."

"Toughs work?"

"Sure. Call them the Eyes. See everyone stays in line. Report back to the Spiffies if they don't."

"Squealers, you mean?"

"That's a mean way of putting it, mate. Spiffies need all the help they can get. Yes, sir. Gotta have law and order. Guess *you* knows that." He gave me a knowing glance, tried a half smile on for size. When I didn't disagree and swat him, I got the rest of it. It didn't stay in place long.

"Bums work too?"

"The easy things. Sweep floors. Pack crates. Things like that."

"How do you become a bum?"

"Too much snifter, get hopped up, can't do their old jobs. Get new ones. Don't pay much. Just enough for snifter, maybe. Only fair, right?"

"Suppose so."

"You betchya. Everyone gotta do his bit in the niche." He looked at me slyly as if waiting for applause.

"What do you do?" I asked.

"Tidy up here in the flop. That's why I'm a scout. Flop-keeps gets to be scouts."

"So what do you think about the niche, Ixil?"

"Me? Think about the niche?"

He turned his head toward the eaters. As if one of them might yet rescue him from this quagmire. Two guys pushed back their chairs and left. They studiously avoided my eyes. I'd wanted privacy. I needn't've worried. At this rate I'd have the whole place to myself soon.

"Sure, there are other niches. Big niches. Small niches. I know that. There are top niches and bottom niches." He wiped the sweat from his forehead with a trembling hand.

"And the Outies are where?"

"Bottom niche."

"You don't mind?"

"Mind?"

"Yeah. Being on bottom."

"Not me. No, sir. That's the way things are. Wouldn't be this way if it was bad. Gotta be good, right?"

I sighed. "Who runs this niche?"

"The Spiffies, mate."

"Where can I find 'em?"

"They're all over. Got their own lookout nests."

I almost knew what he was talking about. "Small buildings between the large ones, eh?"

"Sure."

I made a mental note to avoid 'em. The dining hall meanwhile was emptying out. Time to blow, I figured, before someone smarter than this lad came along and started asking *me* questions.

"The Ul," I said. "Tell me about 'em."

"The *what*?"

"Ul."

"Must be some other niche, mate. Got nothing like that in these parts."

"Ever hear of Magalone?"

He shrugged. "That's a new one on me."

"I suppose Happy City doesn't mean anything either?"

"Can't say it does."

I tried a long shot. "What about the Klarr?"

"What about them, mate?"

"Know 'em?"

"Never heard of them."

"Any strangers like me by here recently?"

"Not that I heard of."

"Not any metal men romping about either, I bet?"

"Metal men?"

"Forget it. What's this world called?"

"The world."

"Anything else?"

"Well, the Great Niche, sometimes."

"Yeah, I can see how you might." I sat back on the hard wooden chair, sighed. "You've done all right, Ixil."

"I have?"

"Uh huh."

"Figured I'd flunked. All them names I couldn't place. Figured I shoulda known them names or you wouldna asked."

"Part of the test," I said.

"And all them things everyone knows. Trying to trip me up, huh?"

"That's how it's done," I said, wondering what I was talking about.

"Sometimes the Spiffies asks us questions. A couple times, an Innie showed up and he asked them. But that's like official, you know. Nothing like this."

"Yeah," I said. "We're getting sneaky."

"That's all?"

"Just about."

"Thank goodness."

I said, "Where do you keep the ladies around here?"

"Ladies?"

"Yeah, you got ladies, right? Visiting privileges too, I bet. What's a niche without ladies?"

He grinned. "Ladies. Sure. You betchya." A lecherous smirk flashed across his face. "Over on the west side. Got their own flops. Pink."

"Pink," I said. I nodded toward the far wall. "That way?"

"Can't miss it. About ten minutes on foot. Less if you gotta bike."

I stood up. "Thanks."

"I passed, huh?"

"Yeah, with flying colors. You're an example for us all, Ixil, a model scout. You'll get ten brownie points for this."

"That good?"

"The best."

"You gonna test some others, too?"

"A few," I admitted.

"Only fair," he said, mopping his brow.

CHAPTER **18**

The streets were crowded with workers pushing off to the plants. No traffic to speak of, just a couple of bicycles. I saw some women, too. Most were dressed like their male counterparts in coarse, unbecoming work-clothes. The Outie niche believed in equal opportunity.

But opportunity for what?

I stuck with the crowd for a few blocks. Not such a hot idea. I wasn't dressed for the occasion. Up ahead, I saw a couple of guys in bright red uniforms. Wide black belts, boots up to their knees, visored caps. They looked spiffy, if not quite as spiffy as me. Nightsticks hung from their belts, but no hardware. I wondered if the population here was especially docile. If Ixil was any example, maybe it was.

I turned, made my way up a narrow alley between two

tall factory buildings. No one seemed to notice. I climbed a wire fence and landed on the other side. I'd had some experience with the back alleys in the Outie niche; they should take me where I wanted to go. I headed west.

As worlds went, I now knew pretty much where I wasn't—namely, all the logical places I might expect to be. This knowledge, somehow, didn't put much bounce into my stride. I was stuck with my Sass theory: that he'd tried a last-minute save and it'd gone haywire. I wasn't crazy about that either. But it was all I had going for the moment. If there was anything in it, Laura and Sass could be stranded here, too. At least I'd have company. And if I ran into Sass, he might actually be able to get us out of here.

I covered about two blocks mulling over this interesting possibility. Then, suddenly, I had other things on my mind.

Two toughs popped out of a side alley up ahead, planted themselves right in my path. They were average height, but with plenty of muscle, wore the calf boots and wide belts that seemed to make up their informal uniform. Their faces held no expression at all. As if they were very bored, or maybe not very bright.

I looked over my shoulder. Just like it says in the Detective's Handbook.

Another identical pair had sprouted behind me, a half block away.

High brick walls were on either side of me. No convenient side alleys led to safety. I was going to be able to see for myself, it looked like, just how docile these lads were.

I thought of telling 'em I was an Innie and bluffing my way through. For all they knew, I could be inspecting back alleys. But I didn't even know what an Innie, in government lingo, was. They might not either, but could I count on it?

My laser was still in my pocket. Fast Draw Dunjer could hold his own against four Eyes. Especially if they were unarmed. Only shooting people on a strange world could lead to more trouble than it was worth. The Detective's Handbook tagged shooting as a last resort. This was no time to ignore the Good Book.

I glanced back again. The guys behind me weren't breaking any speed records to get at me; they were coming on at a slow, steady pace. I put a spring into mine and went to meet the man-made roadblock. What man has made, man can undo.

I got to within five feet of them, pulled up short.

"Want something, guys?" I asked, good-naturedly.

"You, Swellie!"

Swellie?

The shorter of the pair leaped forward. As if to meet the challenge of the Swellie head-on. He spread his arms as though trying to take flight or grab me in a bear hug. The guy was wide open. I put a fist in his face and he fell down.

His pal did a double take, frowned, stepped in quickly with a haymaker right. I got under it, drove a left deep into his midsection.

He went *oof!* and doubled over.

I straightened him with a right. Hooked with my left. And was all set to go to town when he sat down too.

I was so surprised, I almost bent over to help them up. The thought of shooting them was downright embarrassing now. These lads were a danger only to themselves.

I whirled to face the pair behind me, who could've been made of sterner stuff.

They weren't.

The two heroes had slowed to a crawl. They eyed me warily as if I might be a dangerous animal from the zoo that someone had inexplicably let loose. I took a step toward 'em. They began backing up.

Jeez.

I did a hurried about-face, stepped around the fallen gladiators. Whoever taught these guys how to fight had missed some of the finer points.

I continued my back alley jaunt. Glancing over my shoulder, I saw the four in a huddle. They didn't take after me, but started off in the other direction.

I was sorry my mechs hadn't been here to note the brawl. They figured the old man'd gone soft. This would've shown 'em. Especially it they'd seen it from a long way off and couldn't tell what was going on.

I darted across a deserted side street, switched alleys just to be on the safe side. More high walls. A trash can or two. No one got in my way.

Ten minutes later the alley came to an end. I reined up, peered out cautiously. A main drag, this time. It was empty, the workers off at their chores. In the distance, I could see some low pink structures—the lady's flop.

I made sure I was presentable, as befit an Innie, straightened my shoulders, and stepped out onto the street.

Instantly, a flock of Spiffies came pouring out of storefront doorways on each side of the alley, pounced on me.

There were six of them. I could picture more Spiffies covering the other alleys. The Eyes had tattled. At least they were good for something.

A pair of Spiffies held me by the arms. I expected to be padded down for weapons first thing. The Spiffies didn't bother. Here was a bunch who really needed the Detective's Handbook. Too bad I hadn't brought along a spare copy. It would've been worth its weight in gold.

The head Spiffy stationed himself in front of me and glowered.

"Who are you?" he demanded. "And where'd you get that outfit?"

"My good man," I said, staring back at him. "It was all a test, you know." The word had done okay first time around with old Ixil. I had nothing to lose by giving it another shot.

"A test?" He wrinkled his brow. As if I'd said "pile of oozing garbage." I couldn't blame him.

"Most certainly," I said. "What else do you think I'm doing here?"

He gave me another stare. It wasn't suffused with warmth and understanding. "Prove it!" he barked in a voice that would've done a flatfoot on any world proud.

"That is my intention," I said, all dignity. "If you will kindly unhand me?"

I expected to be clubbed for the mere suggestion. I wasn't.

The guy was thinking it over. I must've looked harmless, for he nodded his head. Hands let go of my arms. Jeez.

I reached toward my pocket. "If I may?" I said.

Again the jerk nodded.

By now I was ready to believe they'd never heard of guns on this dumb world. Either that or the Great Niche was a place where they gave all types a crack at the job of their choice. And these types were the mental defectives.

I pulled out my laser. It seemed the smart thing to do. *Someone* had to stick up for smart.

"What's that?" the head Spiffy barked. There was consternation on his face.

I stepped back a pace into the alley. "A laser," I told him.

He frowned. "That's forbidden. Are you crazy?"

I was beginning to think so.

I took another step back. "Just stay where you are," I said, "and no one'll get hurt." The classic statement. Unfortunately, one usually made by the bad guy. I was glad my mother wasn't here to see this.

"Look," the head Spiffy said, "give us that thing and we'll pretend you never had it."

I kept backing up. "Let's pretend I was never here."

"Don't do this," another Spiffy called out. "Use your head."

They stood there, all six of them, gawking at me, their nightsticks dangling from their belts, their hands empty. Spiffy, all right. But useless.

I turned and ran down the alley. Nobody followed me.

CHAPTER 19

I'd have expected an all points bulletin in any halfway sane and rational city-state. (Although, actually, there aren't that many sane and rational city-states, even on my world—maybe especially on my world.) Lawmen would be putting up roadblocks, swarming all over the streets. Communications networks would be ablaze with my description. I had my doubts if the Outie niche had *any* communications network. Maybe smoke signals. And why put up roadblocks for the couple of bikes I'd seen? The Spiffies would probably be sitting around moping about my getaway, rather than out beating the bushes.

Still, I kept a low profile, didn't parade up their main street. The Spiffies acted like sissies, the Eyes like bullies and stoolies. They were authority figures like I was a classical scholar. Something was wrong here, all right.

I just hoped I wouldn't be around long enough to find out what it was.

I left the alley first chance I got, hunted around for a nice quiet side street, one devoid of people. It wasn't hard to find. The tall buildings on both sides of me looked more like warehouses than factories. There were few windows and those were dark.

I peeled off my jacket, slung it over a shoulder, rolled up the sleeves of my blue shirt. The best I could do to look like a native. If anyone got in my way, I could always show them my laser. They'd probably faint.

Again, I headed west.

No one, as far as I could tell, was hanging around outside the double-decker admin flop. The other barracks stretched into the distance. Far off I saw a pair of women policing the grounds.

I rolled down my sleeves, put on my jacket, and hoped I looked like somebody important.

I didn't just walk through the front door. Years of snooping had made me partial to back doors on general principles.

This one was unlocked. I breezed through it, hand on my laser. No welcoming committee popped up to greet me. I let out my breath, let go of my laser, and started on my tour.

If nothing else, this lady's flop smelled better than its male counterpart. Also, it was empty. The bunk beds in the dorms were all neatly made, the cafeteria deserted.

I went up a wide staircase to the top floor. There seemed to be no one here either. I ambled around a bit, poking into broom closets, storage areas, a couple of private rooms that must've belonged to the higher-ups.

None of the doors was locked. Obviously, these folks believed in the honor system. Probably the whole Outie niche had taken the pledge to lay off firearms. Along with swearing, privacy, and higher wages. No wonder the Spiffies were near tears: their system, such as it was, had just gone blooey.

I tried another door. This one opened on to an office. A gray-haired woman sat behind a small desk going through papers. She wore no makeup, was dressed in a workmanlike gray-blue dress, and had a pair of gold-rimmed spectacles perched on her nose.

She looked up from her papers.

"You must be Dunjer," she said. "Come in and close the door."

"My, how I've looked forward to this meeting," she said smiling.

"I was expected, eh?"

"She told me you would come."

"She?"

"Laura."

"She's here then?"

"Was."

"They caught her?"

"Not in the Outie niche. I do not know what happened afterward."

I was plunked down in a cushioned armchair across from her desk. After all my traipsing around this morning it didn't feel half bad.

"She left, eh?"

"Some two months ago."

I looked at her. "That can't be right," I said.

"Two months, three and a quarter days, if you wish

me to be exact. You have been in hiding all this time?"

"I just got here."

Now it was her turn to stare. "I don't believe I understand," she said.

"If you did," I said, "you'd be the cockeyed wonder of the universe, not just this world. How long did Laura stay with you?"

"Four days. She was waiting for you."

"What did she tell you?"

"Everything."

"Must've been a mouthful."

"She told me about Happy City, about Magalone, and about waking up here in the Outie niche."

"Didn't say how she got here, I suppose?"

"She had no idea."

"That makes two of us."

"She is a remarkable woman."

"Yeah," I said. "Even XX41 thinks so, and it's not even human."

"I beg your pardon?"

"Skip it."

She smiled, as though I'd said something smart. "When a scout brought her here, I saw at once how special she was. Not beaten down as are so many of our women."

"You believed her story?"

"It took time for me to fully assimilate what she told me, of course."

"What convinced you?"

"She had a laser, you know. I had never seen one in my life, only heard rumors. It was strong corroborating evidence."

I nodded. "The laser's a great convincer. You're the

boss lady around here, eh?''

"Yes." She smiled. "My name is Qui."

"How come, Qui," I said, "I never got to meet the boss at the men's flop?''

"You wouldn't have liked him; he is a disagreeable person. I do things differently here. I ask to see all the strays. A stray needs guidance, often a good talking to. I feel it is my duty.''

"Lots of these strays are strangers?''

"Assuredly.''

"From where?" I wanted to know.

"This is not the only Outie niche," she said. "There are dozens in this region alone, back to back. A stray from one is always welcome in another.''

"Very hospitable," I said, remembering my own reception.

She nodded. "We want our Outies to be comfortable, after all. There is, as you might imagine, a good deal of crossover. But as the factories are interchangeable, production never suffers.''

Good old production. "Sounds like a swell deal," I said. What it sounded like was prison, but if she didn't know, I sure as hell wasn't going to bring it up. I needed this lady's help. "Where did Laura go?''

"The Science niche.''

"Ah," I said. That made sense, if nothing else did. A science complex, if it were up to snuff, would offer the best chance of getting oriented. "Where's it at?''

"Somewhere in the far north.''

"You don't know?''

"I have never left this area. None of us have. It is unnecessary, you see. As well as forbidden, except under extraordinary circumstances.''

"You're an Outie?"

"I am a supervisor." There was pride in her voice.

"Got a promotion?"

"There are no promotions, Dunjer. I was reared in an Executive niche, a day's journey from here by horse and buggy. I received my training in the Supervisor's niche. As such, I am considered to be a world traveler." She smiled broadly at that. It was a scream, all right. That and the horse and buggy. Something about this conversation was starting to depress me. Badly. As though I didn't have enough to be depressed about.

"Where can I get a map?"

"You can't, I'm afraid. Maps are restricted to the highest levels of government. I myself have never seen one."

"They're lots of fun," I assured her. "Full of squiggly little lines. How did Laura intend to reach this Science niche, use a divining rod?"

"She said you'd ask. There are freight trains not far from here that carry our factory goods throughout the Great Niche. She was planning to board one going north."

"It's called hopping a rattler," I told her. "Anyone can just come along and do that?"

"Gracious, no. The Eyes and Spiffies keep a constant watch at the freight yards."

"Those guys," I said, "seem a bit tame."

"You have seen them then?"

"Uh huh."

"Yes, they prefer persuasion—as do all of us in authority here."

"Sure. You know for a fact that Laura made it out?"

"Your friend is a most resourceful woman. I would have heard if something had gone amiss."

"How do I get to the freight yards?" I asked.

She told me.

CHAPTER 20

I trudged along the main drag.

I didn't have that rotten, neglected feeling anymore. I had plenty of company. The noontime lunch crowd was out of the factories in full force. I was one of 'em.

Qui had dug up some clothes for me that her handyman kept around. I was wearing loose-fitting striped overalls and a coarse gray work shirt. A striped stovepipe peaked cap was pulled low over my forehead, for that extra bit of privacy a guy often wants in large crowds. I'd rubbed some dirt over my neat, self-polishing black shoes, which were, if I knew 'em, polishing away like crazy under the grime.

A hefty tool case dangled from my right hand. No tools were in it. It held a bag of sandwiches, a beverage-filled thermos, and my own suit. The last item would come in handy once I hit the Science niche. Guys who dressed like plumbers might be in scarce supply there. Besides, the suit was expensive and probably unobtainable on this world. If I was stuck here I wanted to be stuck in style.

There were some Spiffies stationed at a couple of intersections, and a few were in the crowd itself, which spilled over the pavement and filled the roadway. The Spiffies appeared glum and dejected, as though the whole unit was sure to be demoted on my account. They didn't seem to be on the lookout for me, either, or anyone else. As if they'd tossed in the sponge once and for all. They almost had me feeling guilty.

The Outies niche was bigger than I'd figured. The main street with its hulking factories kept stretching before me, as if each step I took pushed it a bit further. I didn't mind. As long as my cover held, I was in good shape. Or in as good shape as someone in my fix can be, which actually, wasn't very.

The freight yard was at the street end. All I had to do was keep hiking.

The crowd had been buzzing away, as if lunch break were one large party. The tumult suddenly began to wind down. Movement came to a jerky halt. All talk stopped. Heads, as if governed by a single mind, turned toward the sky.

I looked with the rest. It'd've been rude not to.

At first there was nothing to see. Then I heard the faint whisper of engines. Four specks appeared in the northeast sky. The whisper became a roar as the specks grew in size, turned into jets.

A voice, sounding like a chorus, blared over dozens

of loudspeakers up and down the main street:

"INSPECTION! INSPECTION! RETURN TO YOUR BARRACKS! INSPECTION!"

The damn voice sounded close to hysteria.

The crowd stirred as one, began to scurry off in the direction of their respective barracks. There was terror on their faces. The *real* law, it looked like, was about to put in an appearance. In jets, no less. So much for the horse-and-buggy society I'd been conjuring up in my bean. Something a bit more complicated was happening on this world.

The jets had lost altitude, were coming down somewhere north of the niche.

I scratched the freight yards; they'd do me no good now.

I slipped down an empty side street, pulled the laser from my pocket.

I began to run.

The town started to thin out, the buildings become sparser and shabbier. I didn't know what was in 'em. They looked like logical hiding places. But if I knew it, so would everyone else. Besides, hiding was the last thing I wanted to do. I couldn't outwit the locals on their own turf, once they knew I was here. And the cat was out of the bag. Along with me.

The Outie niche came to an abrupt end and I found myself in a field. Weedlike growths were waist high. I wasn't crazy about that; it made movement too much of a chore. What I liked even less was my exposed position. Out here, I'd be a sitting duck for anyone coming to or going from town. Unless I ran doubled over, or crawled.

Neither prospect seemed like a treat. But not much had recently.

Through a shimmering haze, I could see where the jets had come down—about two, three miles away. Beyond them, far off near the horizon, buildings of some sort were visible. Another Outie niche, probably. Nothing in it for me. Once word of my presence got out, I couldn't count on being safe anywhere around here.

Some trees were about a half mile to my right. They stopped short of the jets, but they'd take me part of the way. Stooping over, as though I had a bad case of intestinal rot, I began trotting for them.

I swiveled my head back and forth between the jets and town as I moved, a tactic better suited for mechs or lunatics. It paid off before my noggin came entirely unscrewed.

Vehicles—a whole convoy of them—began moving from the jets toward town. They didn't waste any time eating up the turf.

I flattened myself on the ground.

Soon they were streaming by on my left, a quarter mile away. Even that was too close. I couldn't tell what was in the covered trucks, but the open cars looked like they held guys nine feet tall. Most were sitting ramrod straight, facing forward, a real credit to their military training. Or lack of curiosity. I bet they could shoot straight, too.

Some of 'em had binoculars and were giving the weeds on both sides of the convoy a good raking. I barely resisted the urge to burrow underground.

They were all wearing silver-black uniforms, with silver helmets. And lugging enough hardware to start a small-scale war. As the only enemy force in hailing distance, I should've been tickled pink by all this fuss. Self-preservation, if not modesty, got in my way, made me wish these lads were hunting someone more deserving than me. A jaywalker maybe.

I figured about three hundred troopers were part of the convoy. All here because I'd waved a laser around. I was glad now I hadn't done anything really bad like spit on the sidewalk; they'd probably have bombed the whole niche into oblivion.

I kept still till the last car was out of sight. Then I pushed ahead toward the trees. I knew it would take 'em a while to comb the town for me. A while, I figured, was all a pro like me needed to come up with something really smart. I could hardly wait to find out what it was going to be.

I lay in the weeds, eyed the jets, and wondered if they'd been worth all this effort. I had my doubts.

The hike through the woods hadn't been half bad. Except for the kink in my back, I was walking tall again.

No one came looking for me. Who would figure I'd head toward the jets and sure trouble, instead of doing the safe thing and hightailing it in some other direction? The military probably, once they'd taken the niche apart brick by brick. Once was still a way off, I hoped.

I climbed back into my Happy City all-purpose suit, ate a batch of sandwiches, stuck a couple more into a pocket, drank up half the thermos, and hooked it onto my belt. The tool case and worker's duds, I left behind. I wanted to travel light.

When the woods ended, I got back on all fours and popped into the weeds again. I crept along bent double like a pretzel for about three quarters of a mile, a real test of character and stamina—one that I almost flunked. If the soldiers hadn't looked so nasty, I might've given myself up then and there. What torture could they cook up that was worse than this?

I finished the thermos, chucked it away, and crawled the last third of a mile.

I lay sizing up the terrain.

The airfield could've handled a couple of dozen planes, it was that big. The four jets were parked far away from each other. Good. It'd make takeoff that much easier— especially if I knew how to fly. A high wire fence was strung around the field. Not so good. I couldn't get to the damn jets even if I *did* know how to fly.

Two soldiers guarded the front gates. Eight others were inside, halfway between the gates and the jets. Pilots and copilots, I figured. They were chatting away, seated on outdoor benches next to a small weathered cabin.

Close up now, I could see the opposition wasn't nine feet tall. Only about seven, give or take an inch. I wasn't reassured. They didn't look any friendlier either.

My plan had been simple: to somehow stow away on one of the jets, lay low till the plane had landed and its cargo of soldiers disembarked, then make my way stealthily into town—wherever that might be—and take up my hunt for the Science niche from there, this time keeping a low profile.

Or better yet, kidnap a pilot and have him fly me directly to the Science niche, at gunpoint.

The fence, guards, and the fact that eight pilots were clustered together made both plans chancy—verging on the downright impossible.

Blasting both guards from my hiding place in the weeds was an idea, only not a very good one. It'd stir up the eight others, who'd probably start shooting back. I wouldn't put it past 'em—they looked nasty.

And how was I going to pry one of those guys loose from his buddies so he could fly me off to safety?

I lay there thinking hard.

A vague image began to form in my mind. I was looking at a control panel inside a jet. The image grew clearer. The panel was automated, I saw. Slowly, a keyboard punched out the words: "Science niche." The monitor screen showed a map. Circled in red was the Science niche.

Not bad, I thought, I've gone insane. My mind had finally snapped under the burden of running Security Plus, of being housemaid to a bunch of metal men.

A rotten place to go bananas, all right. Still, there was a bright side. The troopers wouldn't shoot a crazy man—would they?

I went back to studying the panel in my mind. It was clearer than ever now, a real triumph of lunacy. "Press here for takeoff," the monitor read. I saw myself in the pilot's seat, doing as I was told, pressing the stupid button.

The plane came to life, taxied down the runway, took to the air. Nothing to it. Flying in your bean is a breeze. We jetted along, hopping in and out of fluffy cloud banks.

An eye blink and the Science niche was right under us.

I expected the monitor to flash landing instructions.

Another message popped up: "press eject." Again I followed orders. The cockpit shot into the air—me, naturally enough, with it. A parachute opened above us. We sailed down toward the city below. The only question was, would we live happily ever after? I wasn't going to bet on it.

I lay there wondering what I ought to do. None of my options were worth a damn. I had great faith in the military's thoroughness. And much less in my ability to duck an all-out manhunt. I grinned crookedly, thinking of the jet and my daring getaway. What had gotten into me?

An image sprang up in my mind. I was looking at the cockpit monitor again. "Do it!" was spelled out on the screen.

Jeez, I thought, I really *am* crazy.

"Do it, dummy!" the screen flashed again, turning a bright angry red.

Dummy?

Who did the stupid screen think it was writing at? I had half a mind to show it who was boss. Computerized jets had been on the drawing board years ago in Happy City, before the federal government went splat. None of the city-states could afford 'em now. But that didn't mean they weren't possible.

An automat jet was one I could handle.

"Now you've got it," the screen told me.

Shadup! I thought at the dumb image. But the loony scheme was starting to get to me.

My mind was in worse shape than I'd figured.

CHAPTER 21

It took some doing but I managed to crawl more than halfway around the fence without being spotted. In Happy City I'd've been a cinch to pull down the Great Achievement Award. But in Happy City, I wouldn't't've been in this lousy mess to begin with.

By now I was panting hard, and sweating up a small stream. Little bugs were dancing all over me; they probably hadn't had a playmate my size in years.

I rested a while, took a break, and added up the score.

The troops were still hunting me back in town. A plus.

The monitor in my noodle had clammed up and stopped sending me sage advice. Another plus. I didn't want my mind gummed up with prattle just now—not with my life on the line.

I figured if I hadn't popped my cork completely, the

monitor had to be my old pal, Dr. Sass, stuck between dimensions, back in Happy City, or *somewhere*, doing his best to get me off the hook. Only the little crackpot could pull a stunt like this. But I wasn't ready to take everything he gave me as gospel. His gadgets weren't foolproof, had loused up more than once. For all I knew, he'd misread the jet cockpit.

That would be a minus, all right. But the only way to find out was to go and see.

I was over on the west side of the fence, and to the rear of the closest jet some hundred yards away. The plane's bulk blocked my view of the gate guards, and theirs of me. Just as well, we wouldn't't've liked each other. When last seen, they were thoughtfully facing out toward town. A plus.

The pilots, far over on the southeast side of the field, were, more or less, facing my way. They couldn't see me, though, as long as I kept my head buried in the weeds. A plus, at least till I stuck my noggin out. Then a big minus.

So much for scores. I'd seen better. But the bottom line was still blank. That gave me hope.

I dug my laser out of a pocket, sighted it at the fence, turned the beam to maximum, and pressed the trigger.

The half-inch metal links were thick. But no problem for the old laser, a Security Plus product unmatched in Happy City for heavy-duty work. Twenty minutes, and I'd melted away a good three feet of fence.

I let the gun and fence cool while I raised my head to peer toward town. Nothing doing yet. I peeked at the guards. Their backs were still to the airfield.

The pilots, I saw, were busy chatting.

I readjusted the laser for distance, and narrowed the

beam. Leaning my elbow on the ground, I braced my right forearm with my left fist, sighted on the fuel tank of the jet farthest to the east, and pressed the trigger.

The tank was even thicker than the fence links, but there was a lot less space to cover. I kept the beam fixed on one point.

Four solid minutes crept by—seeming more like thirty—before the metal gave way.

Beam and fuel made contact.

A huge, satisfying roar!

The ground jumped as if ready to run off in alarm.

The jet was gone—a shimmering ball of fire in its place.

Thick black smoke billowed out in all directions, began to spread over the airfield.

I was off and running.

I ducked through the hole in the fence, sprinted toward the nearest jet.

The whole southeast part of the field was filled with smoke, as if a black curtain, shot through with flickering red fibers, had been drawn between me and the pilots. The plane itself blocked me from the pair of guards, who, I figured, had finally turned around.

I ran to the right, past the jet tail. A retractable ladder led up and into the plane. I used it, the body of the plane still between me and the guards.

My scorecard was starting to look brighter. I might even live to play again.

I tumbled into the plane—saw it was empty—shoved my laser back into a pocket, and dashed up the aisle like a track star bent on setting a world record.

I banged open the cockpit door, took a hurried gander.

I couldn't afford to hang around here a second longer if everything wasn't just right.

The keyboard and monitor were staring me in the face, like old trusty pals, delighted at this chance reunion. Sass hadn't given me a bum steer, after all. Nutty, dim-witted laughter filled the cabin—it was mine! I had it coming.

I flipped the On switch, punched out my instructions. The telltale map appeared on the monitor, the Science niche circled in red. Just as it had in my mind.

A panel blinked at me: ACTIVATE?

I gave that a yes on the keyboard.

Behind me I heard the ladder folding into its slot, the door sealing shut.

I plunked down in the pilot seat. It strapped me in. I pushed a final button. The jet seemed to rumble good-naturedly, then began taxiing up the runway, picking up speed.

The plane lifted itself into the air.

The ground grow distant. The airfield became a small rectangle, the men on it mere dots, the burning jet a camp fire, its black tendrils of smoke reaching after me.

Then it all vanished from view.

I grinned, punched out: "maximum speed." I punched out: "evasive action at sighting of aircraft." If this world was anything like Happy City, there might not be any other aircraft—except for the couple of jets I'd left behind. I didn't know. At maximum speed, the latter planes, at least, wouldn't be able to run me down. I'd let the jet worry about any other company that might come our way.

I studied the map on the monitor. The Science niche was next to the Government niche. Beyond it, an Arts niche. Farming niches surrounded the trio.

I chose a distant Farming niche, punched out new landing instructions. I would eject over the Science niche, but the jet would sail on without me, confusing the enemy and buying me time. That was the idea anyway. I hoped the opposition was prepared to go along with it.

I sat back to enjoy the trip.

There were two of 'em and they came streaming out of the north sky. The jet got wind of 'em before I did and veered south.

I snapped out of my reverie, glanced at the radar. Another pair was coming at us from the south.

Scratch the poverty angle, the Great Niche had jets to spare.

My plane began to climb.

That wouldn't do. There was no refuge in the cloud banks. They could track us with their instruments. And I wasn't going to come out on top in a dogfight.

I studied the map. The Science niche wasn't too far off, but I'd never reach it in time. We were over flat farmland now. A patch of hilly, wooded terrain lay in front of us; some green, pint-size valleys were scooped out between the hills.

I punched out my new orders.

The jet continued its climb.

Two new specks appeared on my radar screen. Another pair of jets—this time from the east. Six in all now. Pretty soon I'd be taking on their whole damn air force. Even with my own mechs at the controls, I'd've been sweating bullets. With this alien baby calling the shots, I had only one option, and I was going to use it.

We climbed another five seconds, then broke into a

steep dive. Our descent righted itself, became almost horizontal as we neared the ground. My stomach was busy doing flip-flops. I didn't have time to worry about it.

The opposition was closing in on three sides. The monitor projection had us all meeting in ninety seconds, a party I was determined to skip.

The hills rose up to meet us. I could see the trees, almost note the pattern on the leaves. We whooshed over the treetops, all but skimming them, curved down into a shallow valley which again rose to become a hill.

My jet shot straight up high into the sky, twisting like a corkscrew. And exploded some ten seconds later, right on schedule, as the other jets cut loose with their three-way barrage.

They didn't circle the valley for a last look-see, but took off directly for points due north. Bye-bye, jets.

I watched them go from the valley, where I'd ejected.

I took a deep breath, unstrapped myself from the pilot's seat, stood up on shaky legs, and started walking.

CHAPTER 22

I was getting an eyeful.

The buildings were mostly marble white and multi-shaped: some domed, others flat topped or pointy, and the biggest with plenty of stairs leading up to huge doors, flanked by thick columns; they looked like temples or maybe courthouses—places where you came in on your knees to worship or in cuffs to have the book thrown at you. I was impressed, all right, though neither prospect especially appealed to me. If nothing else they beat the Outie niche by miles, which, it being for Outies, was no big surprise. There was nothing like 'em in the Farming niche I'd tramped through; marble barns would've been impractical anyway. This much classy real estate in one spot would've done even Happy City proud. Or, at least, its landlords.

It was surrounded by a high wall. There were lots of manned gates that would let you into this oasis as long as you had the right I.D. I didn't, but I wasn't going to let that stop me. I had something better. The black, gold-trimmed uniform of a Guardian. Fitting enough, for a keeper of mechs.

I strolled through the east gates of the old Science complex and nobody batted an eye.

The whole region was called the Science niche, but the walled-in area was the lab complex where the work got done. The rest was just shopping marts, glad-times strips, and residential sectors.

No red-uniformed, sissy Spiffies roamed the district. Here, tough, no-nonsense Guardians held sway. I'd conked one on the noodle last night—a guy about my size—made off with his getup. Less than a full day in town and already I'd committed a crime. Who'd believe I'd ever been a security op in another world? I hardly believed it myself anymore.

My laser rested in the guy's holster in place of his projectile gun. All I needed was something to shoot. With my luck I'd probably find it.

I carried a small satchel. Money from the Guardian's wallet had paid for it. It held my suit and the guy's gun.

The astronomy building turned out to be the huge domed structure near the center of town. The citizen who gave me directions looked at me questioningly, as though a guy in my shoes should've known. My shoes were still the Happy City self-polishing kind, but he had a point. I beat it in a hurry, before some real cops showed up.

The employment office was located on the twelfth level. The middle-aged lady in the gray business suit at the director's desk was helpful—wouldn't've dared not to be. She ran through a list of astronomers who'd been hired during the last three months. It took her about three seconds. There were only two of 'em, both guys, and fresh out of school. The way this world was set up, roaming astronomers would be in as short supply as butterflies in winter. In any case, the thought of my Laura—even with all her virtues—qualifying as an astronomer was stretching things a bit.

I asked about techs. The list was longer, but no more enlightening. No one came even close to my nifty sidekick's description. Not so hot. Posing as a tech was an okay cover, one I'd've expected her to try.

"Is this woman a criminal?" the director asked sternly.

I'd wondered if she was going to come up with something like that or just let it ride. I had a hunch most folks here would think twice before asking the law *any* questions. I decided not to club her, nor admit that I was the only criminal I knew about just now, and smiled back instead.

"Nothing like that," I said. "Actually, she's come into some money, and we're trying to track her down."

Safe enough. To say she was wanted might've gotten real lawmen into the act. I had no idea if there were any such things as inheritances in the Great Niche. Either way, this lady, I guessed, wasn't going to call me on it.

"There was someone here who fit her description," she said. "It seems so unlikely, I hesitate to mention it."

"Hesitate no longer," I said.

"One of the cleanup women."

I nodded encouragement. Mostly to me.

"About two and a half months ago."

"Uh huh," I said, feeling even more encouraged.

"I should never have noticed her," the director said. "But she came in here a number of times with her cleaning equipment while I was still on duty. She should have known better. Naturally, I told her that regulations forbid such behavior."

"Naturally."

"She did not seem capable of learning this simple truth."

"The simple truths are often the hardest," I said, bravely using up all the philosophy I'd learned in grade school. "What happened to her?"

"I fired her."

"No less than she deserved." I shook my head. "Doesn't sound like the right one at all," I said. "But I've got to check it out. How can I reach her?" The trick here was not to pant in eagerness and give the game away. I was doing my best.

She shrugged. "Her home address should be in the maintenance pool on the fourth floor."

I gave her a small salute, fought back the urge to say, aye, aye, skipper, and left.

You could still see the marble towers off in the distance, but there was no trace of splendor where I found myself. The streets were narrow, the pavements cracked, and the wooden buildings old and dilapidated. Char ladies and their ilk could've used a good union, all right. Along with a different world.

I'd had to ask directions more than once to get here. My copper outfit was making the few people out on the street nervous. It wasn't doing much for me either. Twice I'd had to dodge a Guardian patrol.

I checked the address again, entered a tottering, ramshackle building, and climbed a dark staircase to the fifth floor. I counted down three doors and used my knuckles.

I waited, was about to try again when the door opened.

She was short and stooped, with stringy white hair, a long chin, and beaky nose. I didn't waste time wondering if this was Laura in disguise. No disguise could be *this* good.

The old crone peered at me suspiciously. "Yes?"

"I'm looking for a young woman," I told her.

"Don't blame you, mister." She cackled.

"This one used to live here," I said.

"Ah," she said, holding the door wide. I stepped into a room that could have been a junkyard. I decided not to sit down.

"You have a name?" she asked slyly.

"Dunjer," I said.

She nodded gravely. "That's the one, mister. Damned funniest name I ever heard of. Your young lady didn't say you was a lawman."

"I'm not."

"That explains it."

"Sure does," I said. "Where is she?"

"Not here. Old Mother Gik got an address for you." She shuffled to a table, opened a purse, returned with a crumpled piece of paper. I took it.

"Where is this?"

"Don't know, huh?"

"Wouldn't ask if I did."

"Not far. Couple blocks east. Can't miss it, whole front porch's fallen in." She chuckled. "You got a nice friend, mister."

"Darn tootin'," I said.

"Took Mother Gik in, gave her this place. Ain't that nice, mister?"

"That's nice," I admitted.

"All Mother Gik had to do, mister, is wait for *you*." She cackled.

"Sounds easy," I said.

"Mother Gik knows how to wait. I done my bit. Now this place is mine, fair and square."

"She paid for it, eh?"

"Money on the line."

I looked around at all the junk. "Enjoy," I said, and went.

I had no trouble finding the address Mother Gik had given me. Even in this neighborhood the building was a standout. The front porch looked as though it had fallen to its knees. The roof was half caved in, and the whole structure was tilting to the side, as if trying to lean over to see if the ground was safe enough to fall on. If Laura had rustled up some dough she wasn't spending it on lodgings.

I looked up at the second floor. No signs of life. The damn ruin looked abandoned. I didn't like that.

The front door was hanging on only one hinge. I pushed it open, stepped into a moldy alcove, went up a rickety staircase. I was feeling less optimistic by the second. As though I'd already found Laura's flat empty.

As far as being a prophet went, I was batting a hundred. And zero, so far, when it came to tracing missing persons.

The door was half open, the place cleaned out. I stood there staring at it stupidly. Whatever good cheer I had left seemed to evaporate, sink through the cracked floorboards, and vanish. I went in to hunt for clues, some secret message she might've left. Nothing doing. I tried the flat across the hall. It was empty, too.

I went down the stairs. I didn't think going back to Mother Gik would get me anywhere. I wasn't sure what would.

The kid was waiting for me outside.

"Spotted you right away," he told me. "From there." He was pointing at the dump directly across the street.

"You live there?"

"Uh uh. No one does. It's where the gang's been watchin' for you."

"Me, eh?"

"Yeah. She said you'd come dressed like a bum, a blue collar, or a Guardian."

"She knew whereof she spoke," I said. "And if I didn't?"

"Then just to follow you."

"That's it?"

"Nah, I gotta ask you your name."

"It's Dunjer, kid."

"Yeah, she said it would be. Some name. Okay, come on."

I came.

CHAPTER 23

I glanced out the window, no mean trick, since Laura was firmly camped on my lap. From her digs on the thirty-first floor, I could see a good part of the city. Not bad. We smooched some more, then just held each other. We'd been doing it for a long time. Deprivation had turned me into a tiger. Not that I wasn't one before.

I was back in my own duds, minus jacket and tie. Laura wore a loose, blue wraparound thing with a yellow sash. The mere sight of it—and her—made me put off all thoughts of cutting my throat, at least for a decade.

Finally, I came up for air. "You really had me going for a while, sweetie," I said, giving her waist an extra squeeze.

She ran her fingers through my hair, gave me a bonus

smooch and dazzling smile. "I knew you'd turn up sooner or later, big guy."

"More than I did."

"Have you no confidence in the great leader of metal men?"

"Not me, sweetie. I know him too well."

"I just wanted to make sure," Laura said, "it was you, dear, and not someone I'd rather not see."

"Which would be just about anyone else on this world."

"Right. So what kept you?"

"Nothing. I only got here a couple days ago."

"That's about two month after me, honey. Where were you in between? Living it up?"

"Tumbling through the universe or something," I said.

"A likely story."

"Whatever hit us, honey," I said, "seems to've scrambled time a wee bit."

She looked at me. "What do you mean 'seems'? And speaking of seems, did you seem to hear any funny voices out there?"

"Yeah. Only they weren't telling jokes."

"Any good quotes?"

"Nothing special. Something about taking over a planet—then the whole galaxy."

"The Klarr," she said.

I nodded. "That's what they called themselves."

"I thought I was imagining it."

"Maybe you were. Maybe we both were. Maybe shooting through the universe that way—or whatever was happening to us—made us imagine things called the Klarr were yakking away, while in reality, nothing was going on.''

''And if it was?'' Laura asked sweetly.

''Beats me,'' I said. ''It's a big galaxy out there, and not even ours. If these Klarr want to grab a world, and then branch out, that's their business. What the hell can we do about it, sweetie? We've got other things to worry about.''

She sighed. ''I suppose you're right.''

''Sure I am.''

''I guess we should get back to us,'' she said.

''Us is the main topic,'' I agreed.

''So, you landed in the Outie niche, too?''

''In the drink *by* the Outie niche. A small, but almost fatal difference. I survived—more or less; I haven't made up my mind which yet.''

''Naturally, the first thing you did then was go searching for me.''

''Who would do less?'' I gave her a hug.

''And that, of course, took you to the lady's flop.''

''They've got a real knack for names on this dumb world, haven't they? I met Qui. A nice old girl—for a junior league despot. And she steered me to the Science niche.''

Laura flashed a smile. ''Now you know why I took all those precautions, sweetie pie. They're all despots on this world. Only most of them aren't nice,'' she said. ''Next you made a beeline for the astronomy building, I bet.''

''Yeah. With some intervening fireworks. You told Qui you'd be in the Science niche, but neglected to tell her *where*, throwing the opposition off base. But, of course, not me. You took the cleaning lady job because that'd give you after-hours access to all the rooms, charts, and libraries.''

"Also, it was the only job I could get."

"A minor detail. You got the director to notice you, so she'd remember when I came looking. And then got yourself fired when you'd done what you'd come for. You knew I'd head for the astronomy building first.''

"It was the only place," she said, "where I could possibly find out where we were.''

"Right. Where are we?''

"Who knows?''

"Great.''

"Thomas, this whole universe is different. It's in another dimension. Magalone didn't appear on any of the star charts, at least not by that name. I never knew where it was to begin with. Did you?''

"Uh uh.''

"So there's no way to know where we are in relation to it now, is there?''

I sighed. "That's what I was afraid of, sweetie.''

"You must fight this fear, Thomas. We can always stay here.'' She waved an arm at the apartment, view, and no doubt the bundle of dough stashed under the bed.

"How come you rate this?'' I asked.

"I pulled a number of jobs, kiddo. As in crime wave.''

"Jeez. You're a public enemy.''

"The public here deserves it. They're too docile. They've let the powers that be run roughshod over them. Anyway, I only knock over institutions, and that's government property—like almost everything on this world.''

"Well, don't count on settling down here just yet,'' I told her. "I'm pretty sure Sass knows where we are.''

"You're kidding!"

"Uh uh. The guy was sending me messages."

She clapped her hands together. "That's terrific!"

"Sorry to cut short your crime wave, kiddo," I said, "but I figure it's only a matter of time before the little guy turns up in person and bails us out."

"I wouldn't count on that," a familiar voice said in my mind.

"Eh?" I said.

Laura and I swapped glances. Both of us had heard it.

"It is only I, the Crystal," the voice said. "And where we are, your Dr. Sass will never find us."

"Where are *you*?" Laura asked, her eyes wide.

I glanced around quickly to see if there were any loose pebbles or pieces of rock on the floor. I didn't find any.

"I am," the Crystal said, "part of you."

"Of *me*?" Laura said.

"Both of you."

"Ech!" I said.

"I had hoped for a friendlier greeting," the Crystal said.

"Nothing personal," I said, "but if I wash my hands, does most of you go down the drain?"

"It's not that simple."

"How about a bath?" Laura said.

"You don't understand. My atoms and yours are intertwined, mingled together; we are one."

"All three of us?" I said.

"Well, that is somewhat of a problem," the Crystal said. "We are one as long as we stay together."

"I don't get it," I said with blinding honesty.

"It is the work of the Destabilizer, you see," the

Crystal said. "Its function was not merely to break things down to their atomic components."

I took Laura's hand. "Spill it," I said. "Let's hear the rest of it."

"We're going to hate it, aren't we?" Laura said.

"I don't see why," the Crystal said. "I can be a great asset in your lives."

"Jeez," I said.

"After things are broken down," the Crystal said, "the Destabilizer reassembles them elsewhere. Now, isn't that a simply wonderful weapon?"

"Hardly sounds like a weapon at all," I complained.

"In time of war," the Crystal said, "the Destabilizer can place troops behind enemy defense shields. By the same token, an enemy attack can easily be blunted by making both the enemy and its weapons *be somewhere else*—far, far away. No one is killed or even damaged. Only dispersed and reassembled. Dr. Trex was a great humanitarian. Although I too, of course, had a hand in this project."

"Mountains," I pointed out, "don't have hands."

"But now that I'm part of you two, I do. Four, in fact."

"Go away," I said.

"I couldn't," the Crystal said, "even if I wanted to."

"We're actually stuck with you?" I said.

"Certainly. The Ul missiles, if you recall, were about to destroy us all. The doctor activated the Destabilizer. The exploding missiles augmented the Destabilizer's power, and, alas, produced an overload. We were all destabilized. Part of my atoms blended with yours. We are now partners for life."

"Life?" I said feebly.

"Oh, what fun we'll have together."

I was breaking into a sweat. "What happened to Trex, the others in the lab?"

"They might have perished. Or perhaps I am part of them elsewhere."

"You don't know?"

"How can I? Proximity is necessary for me to make contact with myself, restore part of my wholeness. I am double, now that you and she are together, but still negligible when measured by my former self. After all, I *was* a mountain. Yet, I retain much valuable knowledge. I was able, for instance, to show you how to fly the jet."

"You, eh? So why the games? How come you didn't just speak up?"

"Too weak. I could only communicate through pictures, and that just barely. Two is *much* better."

"Better for you, maybe," I said. "How'd you know what the inside of the plane was like?"

"I recognized the model. It was an Ul jet."

"They're *here*?"

"I wouldn't know. But their jet certainly is. And from what I have seen of the society here—through you two— it is totally structured along Ul lines. '*Every man in his place.*'"

"That's just dandy," I said. "Halfway around the universe and we're back squabbling with the stupid Ul."

Laura squeezed my hand. "We're outlaws in the Great Niche either way, Thomas. It's nothing to us."

"Oh, but it is," the Crystal said. "Believe me. The Ul can, at least, be reasoned with. But the Klarr are truly savage. If you do not warn the Ul at once, we may all be terminated!"

CHAPTER 24

Laura and I sat rigidly on the couch, our hands glued to each other, as though we'd become a single entity—one that included the rotten Crystal. We'd've been staring daggers at the pesty thing if it were a person or even a mountain. Its just being a disembodied voice in our noodles put us at a slight disadvantage. We stared at each other instead. It had its points, but got us nowhere.

"Look," I finally said, "there's nothing advanced about this society, no way they can have spaceships powerful enough to roam the galaxy. So even if I do manage to tip the top guys that these Klarr are out there, knocking off worlds—and they believe me, a big if—what can they do about it?"

"More than you imagine," the Crystal said.

"My imagination," I said, "must be slipping."

"Allow me to enlighten you," the Crystal said.

"Yeah, be my guest, pal."

The Crystal chuckled in my mind. "While it's quite true that I am much reduced now, it is equally true that a major part of my awareness was dispersed through space."

"So?"

"You *do* remember what happened out there?" the Crystal asked.

"Uh huh."

"Well, so do I. *My* consciousness, however, if you'll forgive me, is *far* greater than yours, is able to perceive realms totally closed to you. The Klarr, as they spoke of their plans, mentally projected the image of the world they wished to conquer. Naturally, I noted this at once, and retained it. When Laura scrutinized the star charts, I instantly recognized the world the Klarr sought— namely this one."

"Quite a coincidence," I said.

"Hardly. We were able to hear them because they were in range."

"In range," I said.

"Hovering near the Great Niche. Where else?"

"Jeez," I said.

"I do believe you're finally getting the picture."

"Getting it? I'm stuck in it! As if just being here," I complained, "wasn't bad enough."

"Have no fear. With the Klarr running things, you won't be here long. No one will, except them."

I sighed. "Didn't happen, by any chance, to spot good old Magalone on that star chart? I'm starting to feel real nostalgic just about now."

"Actually, I did. It's all the way across the universe. Quite unreachable by even the most advanced spaceship."

"So how come," Laura demanded, "we landed *here* of all places?"

The Crystal sighed. "That, unfortunately, I don't know. Perhaps I might if I were still in one piece. But I do know what must be done next."

"Sure," I said, "go warn whoever's top dog on this two-bit world—the Ul, according to you."

"Yes," the Crystal said patiently, "the Ul. The social structure, the jet, all speak of an Ul role here."

"You're missing something."

"Yes?"

"Look," I said, "even if your Ul have been here for six months, rather than just two like Laura, they still wouldn't't've had enough time to take over this world, let alone build a fleet of jets."

"True. But they may have been here somewhat longer. The Destabilizer's effect on time, you know, has never been studied."

"Thomas, why are you arguing with it?" Laura asked.

"Because I don't like where this conversation is heading. The Crystal," I told her, "wants me to walk in on the high and mighty and convince 'em I'm not some kind of a nut case. For that to have any chance of success, the big shots've got to be Ul who were destabilized by Trex's weapon, sent packing through space, just like us, and maybe heard the Klarr, too. That's what the Crystal's counting on. I say, so what? If they already know about the Klarr, they don't need me to tell 'em. If they don't, they'll never buy it, and I'm just putting my neck on the line for nothing."

"You misunderstand," the Crystal said. "Your purpose would be not *merely* to warn them. That would be useless. Left to their own devices, they would be helpless against the Klarr. But with *my* knowledge, the outcome could be quite different."

"I'm supposed to offer your services, eh?"

"To save us all."

"And how do I save myself if they've got other ideas?" I wanted to know.

"I think your friend may have the answer to that."

Laura nodded her blond head. "Yes," she said, "I just might."

CHAPTER 25

I was back in the black and gold trim Guardian's getup, and hating every minute of it. I'd never put much store in mechs as leaders of men, let alone thinking mountains. And here I was letting some piece of rock call the shots.

This whole business with the Klarr was just so much speculation. They could've changed their minds, gone off to do their dirty work in some other dimension, or simply've been a by-product of the Destabilizer, a delusion that the Crystal, for all its smarts, had swallowed hook, line, and sinker.

I'd've ignored the whole thing if it hadn't been for Laura. One of these days, I figured, that woman was going to get me into *real* trouble. And this was beginning to look like the day.

Government Palace turned out to be a huge pink, purple, and yellow domed structure that took up more than three square blocks and looked something like a wedding cake. In a building that size there were bound to be plenty of back and side doors to make a quick getaway through if things didn't pan out. I was just sorry I wasn't using one of 'em now to get into the joint. But I'd been outvoted. Being part of a committee of three, with one of the three an inflated pebble, had its drawbacks.

My uniform had gotten me across the border from the Science niche to the Government niche without incident. My passport, though, ended right here. Or I might actually have made it through the imposing front doors. Purple and yellow uniformed guards stood on either side of them, were on sentry duty at strategic points, patrolled the entire square around the palace. For them I was just another tourist.

So much for the brotherhood of lawmen.

I walked up to the sentry box at the foot of the long marble staircase, nodded at the armed sentry seated inside next to the call box. The damn instrument was the closest thing I'd seen to a phone or communo on this world.

"Who do I speak to about going into the palace?" I asked.

The sentry looked me over. "Let's see your pass."

"I don't have one."

He shook his head disgustedly. "What's wrong with you Guardians? All you guys think you've got special privileges here, right? No pass, no entry. Go through channels, buddy, like everyone else."

"You don't understand," I said.

"Forget it, Guardian. I've been posted here five years; I've heard it all."

"Not this," I told him. I unclipped my holster flap, slowly withdrew the projectile gun with thumb and forefinger, and laid it on the small half-circle platform under his call box. "You'll want this," I said.

The sentry was becoming irritated. "What the hell would I want with your damn sidearm, Guardian?"

I kept my hands in plain sight. "That's just it," I said, "I'm not really a Guardian. I bopped one yesterday and stole his uniform and gun."

The sentry gazed at me with narrowed eyes, waiting for the punch line, sure, no doubt, that I was ribbing him. He did not look amused.

"That's just the half of it," I said smiling good-naturedly. "I blew up a jet in an Outie niche yesterday, swiped another one, abandoned it over a valley where it crashed, and hiked all the way here to give myself up."

The sentry, not taking his eyes off me, began reaching for his rifle.

I raised my hands slowly over my head without being told. After all, I was in the security racket myself and knew the drill. Besides, I didn't want this guy to get trigger-happy and plug me. "Better notify the High Council of State," I told him. "They'll want to see me, find out how I was able to pilot one of those babies. It's classified information, you know." Along with everything else, I was going to add. But I figured he probably knew that already.

The sentry touched a button on his call box, while keeping his rifle trained on me with one hand. Daring. A siren began to wail. The patroling sentries started running toward us, their rifles unslung and at the ready.

"Tell 'em I'm from Magalone," I said helpfully. "They'll want to know that."

"Shut up," he said.

They frisked me, hauled me into the palace, and frisked me again. A captain of the guards heard the few words of wisdom I was willing to utter, went away, returned presently looking grim, as though he'd discovered I was the dreaded plague carrier they'd all been warned against, and had me deposited in a windowless room deep inside the palace.

I sat and waited.

I was pretty sure the mention of Magalone would do the trick. The Ul weren't likely to forget their deadly enemy. Provided, of course, there were any Ul around. If I was dealing just with Great Nichers, I didn't have a prayer.

The door opened and a short man waddled into the room. He was alone.

He wore a purple, black, and yellow uniform, with lots of gold braid and piping. A half dozen medals decorated his chest. A gun barrel stuck out of a holster attached to a black belt. He kept fingering it nervously.

I looked at him, raised an eyebrow. His once slicked back, shiny black hair was all but gone. What little he had was either gray or white. As if to make up for this loss, his paunch had grown, become a jutting belly. His sharp-featured face sagged a bit, was fuller, rounder, over a double chin.

He peered at me nearsightedly, his hand now permanently attached to his holster, keeping his distance—as if maybe I *did* have the plague.

"What do you know about Magalone?" he whispered

harshly. There was a quiver in his voice.

"Either this climate doesn't agree with you, Guver," I said, "or you've been living it up a mite too much."

His voice shook. "Guver? Where did you hear that? My name is Irk."

"Not an improvement," I told him.

He tried to draw his belly in, stand erect. "I am General Irk, Commander of State Security. Do not trifle with me. *Who are you*?"

"Dunjer's my name, and security's my game. I'm the guy who pulled your plug back on Magalone, remember?"

His mouth came open. "What?" he said as if suddenly gone deaf.

"Wake up, pal! The Ul attack. The explosion. The trip through space. You haven't forgotten so soon, have you? Dunjer, of household mechs: 'Let a strong metal hand do your chores for you.' Me and my mechs ran you down in the tunnel, brought you up to Trex's lab. Just before all hell broke loose. Ring a bell now, or are you still napping? Dunjer, pal, Dunjer."

His face had turned an interesting shade of chalk white. "D-D-Dunjer?"

"Hey, I think you've got it. Yeah, Dunjer, in person. Accept no substitutes."

Guver shook his head from side to side as though trying to ward off a flock of insects. "His son, maybe, his grandson—"

"Come off it, Guver, this is no time to play games. The Klarr—those voices you heard in the universe—are planning to take over this world. And I'm the only guy who knows how to stop 'em. Go scout up the High

Council, get 'em to give me a listen. There may not be much time left. Go!''

The guy's mouth was still open, his eyes bulging. He staggered back on legs that shook, fumbled for the doorknob, and backed out of the room. I hadn't made this much of an impression since my car stalled on Happy City's main drag last year and tied up traffic for fifteen minutes during rush hour.

The Crystal sighed. "I had hoped," it said, "to encounter myself, you know.''

"In Guver?"

"Certainly, where else?"

"No luck, eh?"

"There is nothing there, only Guver.''

"Or what's left of him," I said. "Not that he was so hot to begin with. What happened?''

"I honestly don't know. Perhaps he was standing too far away from me when the lab exploded.''

"When did the guy land here?" I asked.

"Long before you.''

"Glad you know *something*.''

I cooled my heels some more, mentally going over the speech I planned to make. A lot was riding on it. I felt like a kid going for his first job interview.

When the door opened a second time, Guver wasn't alone.

Six men filed into the room with him. Three were middle-aged, two young, and one as old or older than Guver. All six wore long pink and purple robes.

I was a bit surprised. I'd figured the guards would show up to haul me before the High Council. Instead, the High Council had come before me.

"On your feet!" the youngest looking one barked.

I rose. Now we were all standing. Mine had been the only chair.

"You are in the presence of the High Council of State!" the young one yelped at me.

"Yeah, I know. I bow?" I asked. "Or will a friendly nod do?"

"Your disrespect has been noted!"

I shrugged. "Just asking." Already I was getting off to a bad start.

The oldest one spoke. "You will answer our questions."

He had the deep, resonant voice of a politician. A portly, silver-haired gent with a large nose, full lips, and wide brow, he was the tallest of the six. His shoulders were wide, but age had put a slight stoop to his back. As if the burdens of state had proved heavy indeed.

"That's what I came for," I assured him.

"I am Gem, Supreme Potentate," he said.

"Dunjer," I said. "Fresh off Magalone, previously from Happy City. You wouldn't know the last one."

"I do not know the first one," Gem said, creasing his wide brow. He eyed me sternly. "Where are you from?"

"Where did you learn to fly our jet?" a skinny, middle-aged council member demanded, raking me with his eyes.

At least I had their attention. I wasn't so sure it was an asset.

I looked at them, each in turn. "Let's not beat around the bush, gentlemen. Odds are, some, if not all of you, are UI. And, if not, Guver here," I nodded at the man calling himself Irk, "can verify what I say; he comes from Magalone, too. I've got no argument with the UI,

174

incidentally. I was hired by Magalone to catch spies, not fight in their war. All that, in any case, is past history now. We've got a bigger problem facing us.

"If you guys *are* Ul, I know you didn't plan on coming here any more than I did. We were hijacked when Trex's weapon and the Ul missiles collided. But if you and I were on the same trip, some of you probably heard the voices, too."

"Voices?" Gem said, a half smile on his face.

"I'm talking about the Klarr, Supreme Potentate. They come from their own universe, and they want this one, too, beginning with your world. Maybe you thought you were imagining these voices. Maybe you felt there was nothing you could do to ward off their attack. Well, you were at least right about the second part—till I showed up. I can give you the know how, show you how to beat back the Klarr, and save this world. It's why I took the risk of giving myself up, of placing myself in your hands. We've all got to work together, or it's curtains for this world, and maybe the rest of your universe, too. What do you say, guys, we got ourselves a deal? You gonna give me a chance to do my stuff? Whaddya say?"

The guys didn't say anything. They just stared at me.

Gem slowly turned to Guver, as if my speech had aged him even more.

"Irk," he said, "what is this man talking about?"

Guver shrugged.

"Who are these Ul?" Gem asked.

Guver spread his hands. "I have never heard of them, Your Greatness."

"The Klarr?" Gem said.

"Nor them."

Gem exchanged glances with his council. "Has anyone?"

They all started to shrug, as if fleas had suddenly penetrated their garments.

"He is obviously insane," the thin council member said.

Gem nodded. "Obviously," he said.

"Or lying," the youngest one said, "for reasons of his own."

"We will find out which," another said.

"Listen, guys—" I began.

Guver stepped to the door, flung it open. Guards filled the doorway.

Gem glared at me. "Your childish deceptions are futile. And offensive."

"Everything I told you was true," I said. "And Guver knows it! Where did he come from? Have you ever looked up his records? Ask him—"

"Silence!" one of them screamed.

Gem said, "We shall allow you time to reconsider. A very short time. Should you fail to do so, you will be subjected to a *scientific* interrogation. You will not enjoy it. In fact, few have survived the ordeal." He eyed me significantly. "It is your choice."

CHAPTER **26**

"Some choice," I said.

I was in a small, dank cell somewhere in the palace basement. There was no window, which was probably just as well—it would only've looked out on a blank wall; I had four of my own and they did nothing for me. One dim light bulb glowed feebly on the ceiling. I sat on the floor, my back against the wall. The wall seemed damp, or maybe I was sweating.

"An invaluable experience," the Crystal said.

"Sure," I said. "You're not going to be 'scientifically' interrogated, are you?"

"Were I in your place, I shouldn't mind at all. Rocks, you know, don't feel pain. And, in a manner of speaking, I *am* here. A witness perhaps to your very last moments.

Which I do hope are not too unpleasant. I can't abide screaming.''

"I'll try and remember.''

"However, we *do* have a very nice little rescue plan hatched up, don't we?''

"Rescue plan,'' I grumbled. "We wouldn't need one if you'd listened to me. I told you my waltzing in here wouldn't get us anywhere.''

"But it did. We now know Guver is here. And that he's lying.''

"It's what the guy does best.''

"Ah, but why hide the truth now? Have you asked yourself that?''

"Not recently. Maybe I've got other things on my mind.''

"The social structure, as we have seen,'' the Crystal said, "is Ul. No phones, no newspapers, radios, or 3-Ds; no way to communicate within the niche, let alone interniche communication. But Guver, whether an Ul himself or an Ul agent, could hardly, acting alone, have transformed this world in the relatively short span he has been here. Is he then the leader of some vast Ul conspiracy, permeating all of society? Is that why he seeks to mask his identity from the High Council? Or is he perhaps the last of the Ul, most of whom, having landed before him and done this work, are now dead?''

"No little Uls to carry on, eh?''

"To be transported here, the Ul would have needed to be near the Destabilizer.''

"So?''

"Only their attack force was. All male. Perhaps they could not mate with the native population?''

"Who gives a damn?''

"We do."

"Speak for yourself, chum. I couldn't care less."

"You are being pigheaded, Dunjer. Without the council's help, the Klarr will triumph."

"They may do that anyway."

"Don't be a defeatist. Guver is the key. What we need is leverage. Something to make him talk."

"What we need is to get me out of here."

"That may happen any moment."

"Yeah?"

"If not sooner."

"You know something I don't?"

"Many things."

"Aside from those."

"What I can tell you is that I feel myself growing more complete."

"I can hardly stand the reduced version."

"Greater. Mightier. More me like."

"Jeez."

"I honestly expect the door to open any second."

"It won't be the palace guards, eh?"

"Come now."

The door opened.

Laura stuck her blond head in, winked at me. "This is really a very unpleasant dungeon," she said.

"Holding block," I said. "They prefer holding block, I think." I got to my feet. "What kept you?"

"Kept me? All things considered, I made splendid time. It's no cinch pulling a jail break. Here." She tossed me a bundle. "Your suit. Better than the uniform—they'll be looking for that."

"Both parts gloriously reunited," the Crystal said. "Me. I. Us. If still somewhat circumscribed."

179

"Somewhat," I said. I climbed out of the uniform and into my good old Happy City product. The Crystal wasn't the only one who was feeling more complete.

I went into the corridor, stepped over the prone figure of a guard. "You bump him off, sweetie?"

"Stunner," Laura said. "From my crime workshop. The Crystal's brainchild."

"Not bad for an ex-mountain," I said.

"I told you everything would be all right," the Crystal said.

"You call this all right?"

Laura silently handed me a laser.

"You just stun 'em," I said, "but I get to kill 'em, eh?"

"Man's work," she said.

We moved up the dim cell block, past locked cell doors and an occasional sprawled guard.

"Any problems?" I asked.

"Only the usual. Philosophical. Ethical. And moral. Otherwise, our cubes opened all the doors without a hitch. Just as I predicted."

"And I," the Crystal chimed in.

"You two ought to go into business together."

"But to get at the doors," she said, "I had to stun some guards."

"Showed 'em your legs, eh?"

"Stun, not enchant. I put my kids on the job—the ones who'd been watching for you, kiddo, in the slums."

"Your bunch of juvenile delinquents and partners in crime, eh? Corrupt 'em while they're still young."

"It doesn't matter," the Crystal said. "Everything here is organized by the state. Even crime. Her young lads are simply the first true independents."

"Inspirational," I said.

"I had them distract the patrols outside the palace," she said. "They threw stones. The guards gave chase. I sneaked over to a side door, stunned the only guard left, used a cube, got inside, and dragged the guard after me. That was the hard part, Thomas. Finding you was child's play. The Crystal simply sought itself out and gave me directions."

"I am attracted to myself, you know."

"Enamored," I said.

"The Crystal," Laura said, "was kind enough to brief me on what happened with you and Guver."

"When?"

"Now."

"Whadda blabbermouth."

"Cheer up," she said, "I know just where to go."

"For what?"

"Leverage."

We stepped over another guard, came to a staircase, and crept up the stone steps. No one stopped us. A door was at the top of the stairs, a snoozing guard propped up against it.

Laura used her beeper, one of the two on the whole planet as far as I knew. "What's happening?" she asked.

"All clear out here," a young voice answered from the second beeper. "Patrols still chasing our men."

"Boys," I murmured, "not men, boys."

"Hurry," the voice said.

We reached the door, pushed it open, and peeked out into darkness. Night had fallen.

"They don't know about stunners on this world," the Crystal said. "Introducing stunners, beepers, and lasers to these lads could ultimately subvert the entire social order. You two are revolutionaries.''

"Some way to earn a living," I complained.

"Thomas, stop arguing with it. Let's go!"

We stepped into the night. And beat it. Leverage, here we come.

CHAPTER 27

The National Archives Museum was stashed near the freight yards in a northwest corner of town.

Once, this area had probably been a live wire. Now it was a discarded relic of times gone by. No cops or stray walkers were on the prowl here among the warehouses. We had the place to ourselves.

"Spooky," Laura said.

"Yeah, all that's missing is the tombstone."

I glumly examined the peeling building that housed the museum. It was sealed tight. Huge strips of tin were nailed over front door and windows. We began working our way around to the back.

"A true anachronism," the Crystal was saying. "A storehouse of history, and the Great Niche prefers its subjects ignorant of history."

"Along with everything else," I said.

"Except their duties in the niche, of course," the Crystal said.

"Keeps 'em out of mischief," I said.

"No doubt the archives were sealed soon after the new era began—too soon for Guver to appear in them, wouldn't you think?"

"Maybe."

"Better by far," it said, "are the State Security files in the army fortress. We should go there at once!"

"After you, pal."

The Crystal sighed. "For locomotion," it said, "I am entirely dependent on you."

"A real drawback," I admitted.

The back of the building faced a darkened warehouse. It looked like an okay spot to get busy. I got a cube out, checked for alarm systems. There weren't any.

"The Ul didn't take over this world in a day," Laura told the Crystal. "There may very well be some data on Guver here. Or his friends, even. You have no way of being sure. Leverage could come in many forms and guises."

"They will be looking for you, for *us*," the Crystal objected. "Why not do the smart thing—go directly to the heart of the matter, namely the security files?"

I dug out my laser, began working on the layer of tin that covered a back window.

"Simple," I said. "Breaking into their army fortress is out-and-out suicidal. This is just chancy, a big difference."

"But we may learn nothing here."

"Can't have everything," I said.

* * *

There was plenty of dust.

The interior of the museum looked as though it hadn't been used in decades. We'd tramped through the whole joint, giving it a quick, and futile, once-over before settling on the periodicals room.

Laura and I were seated on either side of a long dusty table piled high with bound volumes of yellowing newspapers we'd collected from the stacks. We'd been digging through them for the last half hour. Every other page all but crumbled at our touch. No follow-up sleuthing on this job, we either spotted our data first time around or lost it.

Skimming through the old news stories was not proving a heartening experience.

The old order had been nothing to brag about. A centralized government under a guy called Plf the Third, it could've given the Ul lessons in bloodletting. This Plf kept his cops, soldiers, and secret police on the go, snaring dissidents, agitators, and subversives, who, if you believed Plf's press, numbered in the millions. The prisons were full and more were being built every day.

The papers had been running their usual uplifting arrest and execution pieces when they suddenly stopped publishing, as if newsprint had dried up overnight. No hint of why was in the last paper. Next day's might've told the story, but there was no next day's. Or any other publications for that matter.

"Whose turn is it now?" Laura asked. She sneezed. A nice dust smudge decorated her left cheek.

I sighed. "Mine."

I trudged into the hallway, made my way to the

stacks, four doors down, pulled open a drawer in one
of the cabinets, and began lifting out another volume
of papers.

"No," the Crystal said.

"No, what?"

"These are only three years older than the last."

"What's wrong with that?"

"You must go back further."

"Look, chum, Guver didn't pop up on this world as
a toddler. He was already middle-aged on Magalone.
Going back forty years is pushing it; any more and we've
lost him for sure."

"Sixty years is the place to look."

"Sixty?"

"Guver, if you recall, wasn't the only one in that lab."

"So?"

"As I have already pointed out, the Destabilizer's
effect on time has never been studied."

"You're telling me that instead of hundreds, we've
got thousands of papers to sift through?"

"Precisely."

"Oh, boy."

"Thomas."

"Eh?"

"I think we've found some of our people."

"People?"

"Mechs."

I put aside the worthless volume I'd been scrutinizing,
reached for hers.

It was a small story on page nine of the *Daily Truth*.
MECHANICAL MONSTERS HUNTED DOWN the headlines
read. These monsters, the story said, had come off

some mad scientist's workbench—spurred on by crazed antistate elements—to rain havoc and terror on the peaceful empire of Plf the Second. Fearless army units had engaged the marauders and made short work of them.

"Not without a fight," I murmured grimly.

"The poor guys," Laura said.

"If we don't hurry," the Crystal said, "we may be next."

I sighed, went back to turning pages.

"Hmmmmm," I said.

"Is that positive or negative?" Laura asked.

"I don't know yet. Take a gander at this."

I shoved the volume across the table, creating a small dust storm.

She peered at the picture. "It *could* be Trex."

There were twelve guys in the photo, half of 'em grinning, all wearing lab coats. The caption read: SCIENTISTS FOUND PHYSICS INSTITUTE. The small story underneath explained that the government of Plf the Second had granted a rare charter to the Jrb Institute, a private outfit, in recognition of their service to the state.

"Guy doesn't have a mustache, and his name's Jrb," I pointed out.

"On this world," Laura said, "a silly name like Trex would have had them rolling in the aisles."

"Also," I said, "he looks a lot older than Trex."

"He *is* a lot older," the Crystal said. "It is the doctor, however, beyond doubt. If I don't know him, who does?"

"Must've come down here in prehistoric times," I said.

"Certainly well before Guver," the Crystal said.

"Doesn't help us much," Laura said.

"Don't be so sure," the Crystal said.

"Look," I said, "the guy's probably been dead for years."

"Even dead," the Crystal said, "the doctor should not be underestimated."

"The strain of no longer being a mountain," I said simply, "has become too much for you."

"The Jrb Institute still exists," the Crystal said. "Its name was listed in the astronomy building as a sister organization."

"I don't remember it," Laura said.

"But *I* do," the Crystal said. "I remember *everything* you glanced at—even in passing. No doubt the institute has long since been taken over by the current government. But it's not located in the science complex. It is on the outskirts of the Science niche, probably in its original building. That will make it easier for us."

"Nothing will make it easier," I said.

"Trust me," the Crystal said. "We must examine the Jrb records. The doctor kept extensive notes. I know, for I was their receptacle. If he lived into the Great Niche era, there may well be vital information about Guver or the Ul in his private papers. While it's still dark, we must break into the Jrb Institute and find them."

Laura said, "And if they're not there?"

"Other records will be, that will help us track down his associates," the Crystal said. "The youngest may still be alive, and able to help us."

Laura and I looked at each other through a haze of dust.

"You game?" she asked.

I shrugged. "Anything's better than this."

CHAPTER 28

"Dr. Stp?" I said.

"Eh?"

"That's your word," Laura said.

"Don't worry," I said. "I'll get it back before we go." To him I said, "Got a moment?"

He was wearing a brown robe over green pajamas, and black slippers. "Sure, who're you?"

"We're from the Bureau of Records."

"Didn't know there was one."

"There's one of everything in the Great Niche," Laura said, "even if it doesn't work too well."

The oldster chuckled, held open the door, and invited us in. "Retirement Haven," he said, grinning. He gestured us to a sofa. "Sit," he said, plopping into an easy chair.

We sat.

There were plenty of expensive, if worn looking, furnishings in the one-room flat. A thick rug lay underfoot. Books lined three walls.

"Books," I said.

"Preniche," he said.

"They let you keep them?" Laura asked.

"Long's I keep 'em to myself."

"Because of your advanced age?" she said.

" 'Cause the Jrb Institute did the state a service."

"Under Plf the Second," she said.

"Yep."

"What kind of service?"

"Invented a new type automat projectile weapon."

"What's it do?" I asked.

"Kills folks lickety-split."

"Impressive."

"If you get a rear outta killin' people."

"The Great Niche grateful, too?" Laura asked.

"They let me be. All of us from Jrb. Not many left."

"That's what we've come about," I said.

"The institute?"

"Jrb."

"The old man?"

I nodded.

The oldster stopped grinning, looked at us closly. "There isn't any record bureau, you know. Just secret police files. Hardly the same thing."

"We got your address," I said, "from the Jrb Institute. About two hours ago."

"Place isn't open then."

"We broke in."

"Don't say?"

"We're looking for Jrb."

"I can direct you to the cemetery."

"Or," Laura said, "his personal papers."

"How'd you know he left any?"

"The doctor," I said, "made a habit of keeping extensive notes."

"The doctor?"

"Right."

"You talking about long ago?"

"Uh huh."

"How long?"

"Very."

"Musta looked kinda different then, I bet."

"Had a mustache."

"What about his name? That the same?"

"It wasn't Jrb."

"What was it?"

"Trex."

"Darned!" he said. "You got it!"

"We get the prize, eh?"

"Sure do. Old Jrb, you know, made us all memorize that darn fool word."

"Trex."

"That's the one. Along with the mustache. Swore us to secrecy. Said someday, someone might show up askin' for him. Just about gave up hope, too. Not that it matters much, I guess, after all these years."

"You never know," I told him.

Laura smiled. "And we get the papers?"

"Don't know about any papers. What you get is Vlg's address."

"Vlg's address?"

"He was the youngest of the whole bunch. Doc passed

the whatchamacallit to him, I reckon.''

"What whatchamacallit?''

"Beats me. The doc, he never did say. I'll tell you one thing, though.''

"What's that?''

"Better get yourselves some bikes.''

"Bikes?''

"Old Vlg lives way out in the sticks.''

"Sticks?''

"Southeast Farm niche. Nice country setting. Some of the Jrb big shots got to live out there. It's the reason, I reckon, he got to hold the whatchamacallit.''

"Because he lives out there?''

"Sure. What other reason could there be?''

CHAPTER 29

It was a red-roofed, white frame cottage. Green fields stretched to the south, bluish hills to the east.

We parked our bikes—for which Laura had plunked down a nice wad of cash—against a tree, walked up the gravel path. The sun had risen. It was mid-morning.

I used the knocker, waited. My knees felt unhinged and I wondered if I was going to fall down.

"Mind if I lean on you, kiddo?"

"You," she said, "are sadly out of shape."

"Sadly," I admitted. "Last time I rode a bike, I was in grade school." I thought it over. "Wasn't in such hot shape then either."

"We could have," she said, "hijacked an army vehicle."

"Yeah, and had 'em all breathing down our necks.

Being honest," I told her, "builds character." I held up a hand. "I know, it's too late in my case, eh?"

The door opened.

The woman who stood in the doorway was middle-aged, clad in a long, black polka-dot dress. Her blond hair was short, her oval face pale. She had large brown eyes.

I asked for Dr. Vlg.

She lowered her gaze. "My father died last year."

"I'm sorry to hear that," I said. More sorry than she could imagine.

"Perhaps he left something for us?" Laura said.

"Left something?" The woman seemed genuinely puzzled.

"Dr. Stp sent us," Laura said.

"Yes?"

"It has to do with your father's old boss, Dr. Jrb," Laura said. "He had a mustache at one time. And his real name was Trex. Does that tell you anything?"

The woman stared at us. By the look in her eye, I figured what it told her was that we were crazy. Then her brown eyes seemed to flicker, come into sharper focus. She peered at us, quizzically, as if gazing at a pair of peculiar animals at the local zoo. "Can you tell me," she said hesitantly, "where Dr. Jrb originally came from?"

"Magalone."

The woman nodded. "It's been so long . . . ." she began. "Believe me, this has been the last thing on my mind."

I believed her.

"Wait here," she said, turned, and went into the house.

It took a while. I spent the time trying to imagine what we'd do with a trunk full of papers. It did not bring unbridled happiness into my life.

I needn't've worried. When the woman returned, all she held in her hand was a thin yellow envelope. She gave it to me without a word, her lips set in a hard line.

"That's it?" I said. "No packages, no boxes, nothing else?"

She shook her head. "This is all he left."

I looked at the damn thing, turned it over a couple of times. "Thanks," I said, slipping it into a pocket.

"It's illegal, isn't it?" she burst out. "All of this."

"Search me," I said. "I've no idea what's in here."

"It has to be," she said, "with all this secrecy."

"Maybe," I said.

"If they catch you," she said urgently, "don't tell them where you got it."

"It's okay," Laura said. "He stands up quite well under torture."

The thing went beep.

"It beeped you," Laura said.

"Probably just being friendly."

The thing, which had come out of the yellow envelope, was flat and round like a coin, and fit into my palm. It had a needle like a compass, but it wasn't pointing north. It pointed east, toward the bluish hills. It beeped frantically when you tried to point it in any other direction. I stopped trying.

"Has a mind of its own," I said.

"Like its inventor."

"You'd think," I complained, "he'd've at least left a note."

"The right finders wouldn't need a note," she pointed out.

"In their absence, I suppose we'd just better follow the needle."

I looked around for a handy bus, trolley, or taxi that might carry us in style. There weren't any.

We climbed back on our bikes and began pedaling east.

"There are times," the Crystal said, "when not having legs is a decided advantage."

I extended a hand to Laura, helped her scramble up on the ledge.

She stood next to me panting. I panted right along with her. What were friends for?

We'd found a couple of dirt roads that took us halfway to the hills. When the roads gave out, we hid our bikes in a thicket, set off cross-country on foot. The fields brought us to a wooded incline that led to the base of the hills. The thing was now beeping us madly toward the northeast. We climbed in that direction, guided by needle and beep, till we hit the ledge. Join Security Plus, get to have fun.

I dug the gizmo out of a pocket, gave it another look-see. The needle was parallel to the ledge.

"Good news," I said. "No more climbing. It's back to jolly old hiking."

"I bet there's bad news, too."

"Yeah. The hiking's along the dumb ledge."

It wasn't exactly a hike. The ledge varied in width from three feet to one. We crept along, our fingers clutching desperately at the hillside.

It took us ten minutes to reach the opening. I kept

going a step. A beep sounded from my pocket.

"Master's voice," Laura said.

I pulled out the doodad. Its needle pointed directly at the opening.

It was no more than a shrubbery-covered hole in the rocks, just large enough for someone to crawl through. We were the only someones in the vicinity.

I said, "There'd better be an easy chair, a tall drink, and some tasty snacks down there."

"Would you settle for Trex's notes?"

"Only if I have to."

I fished out my Security Plus pocket flash. "After me," I said. "As president of this outfit, I get to go first."

"In case there *is* a snack down there?"

"Right. Better get your laser out, sweetie."

"In case something's down there that wants to snack on us?"

"Right, again. May be crashing some creature's living room."

"I'm afraid," the Crystal said.

"Eh?"

"It said it was afraid," Laura said.

"I heard what it said. Look," I told it, "I've gotten you this far, haven't I?"

"It's not that," the Crystal said.

"What is it then?"

"I don't know."

"Great."

"There, there," Laura said soothingly.

"I really don't feel well at all," the Crystal said.

"Jeez."

I crawled into the hole, Laura at my heels. It widened at once. We got to our feet, moved along a narrow passageway that led deep into the hill. Our footsteps sent echoes bouncing back at us. My flash crisscrossed the walls, revealing nothing.

We walked upright most of the way, bent double once, and—during the last stretch—crawled on hands and knees.

"How you doing?"

"Me?" Laura said. "I'm almost hysterical."

"Crawling in caves will do that," I explained calmly. "That's probably why *I'm* almost hysterical. But, actually, I meant the Crystal."

"I can't breathe," the Crystal said.

"Mountains don't breathe," I reminded it.

"Helllp!" it wailed.

We straightened up again. The passage grew bigger, wider, became a bona fide cave. I took a deep breath, shone my light around. There were plenty of shadows but not much else.

"See anything?" I asked.

"Thomas, over there."

"Where?"

"Straight ahead. Something glittered for a second."

I raised the flash. "Nice outcrop of rock," I said.

"Beyond it."

We moved ahead, slowly, purposefully. Something that gleamed could be metal. Metal could be a trunk. A trunk could be full of papers. Just what we wanted. But that many papers would take hours to sift through. We'd starve first.

"We're doomed," I said. "We forgot our picnic lunch."

It wasn't a trunk, though.

It was the Destabilizer.

CHAPTER **30**

We stood there transfixed, staring at the damn thing. It was identical to the original weapon, long nosed and tapered, somewhat like a cannon. It had its own monitor with a single row of keys. Only the pedestal and seat were absent.

I raised the flash higher. A pint-sized version of Trex's lab computer gleamed back at me. Vectors, dials, gauges, multicolored light bulbs, two screens. For all the life in 'em, they might've been a painted picture.

"No records," I said.

"No leverage," Laura said.

"No snack even."

"Thomas, what's it good for?"

I shrugged. "Destabilizing things."

"What's to destabilize down here?"

"Nothing."

"We must . . ." the Crystal said, "we must . . . see if it works."

"Why?" I asked. "You wanna shoot someone?"

"It does . . . not shoot," the Crystal gasped.

"Sure, it destabilizes. So what?"

"Trex was . . . a genius."

"Yeah, I know," I grumbled. "He wouldn't've wasted his time if there wasn't a damn good reason. So what's the reason?"

"I don't understand his motives . . . but I am . . . I am not at my best . . . . Please—"

"Thomas! Do what it wants."

"What I want," it gasped, "is to lie down."

"I'd be glad to oblige," I said.

"Go . . . go to the weapon," it croaked.

Laura grabbed me by the arm, dragged me over to the contraption.

"Press the left key," the Crystal whispered.

I pressed. Nothing happened.

"Maybe it's not plugged in," I said.

"Where's to plug into?" Laura asked with piercing logic.

"*Arrrrrg!*" the Crystal said.

"What kind of an answer is that?"

I didn't get to ask any more. Something seemed to reach out of the darkness around me, send me spinning. I tipped sideways like a large—helpless—jug of water, crashed to the ground. Like water, my consciousness splashed away from me. I was in a swirling pool of darkness. I sank down into it. A tiny pinpoint of light glistened overhead. It vanished too, and there was nothing.

* * *

My eyelids felt leaden. I could hear footsteps, echoing voices from somewhere around me. It took some doing, but I managed to pry open an eye. Dim light shone from somewhere. I was lying facedown on the floor of the cave, Laura stretched out by my side. Her eyelids flickered, came open slowly. Her hand reached out, squeezed mine.

A voice was saying, "It doesn't even work."

Another, more distant voice said, "It is unfinished then?"

"Obviously."

I rolled over, groaned, put an arm out, and levered myself up into a sitting position. It wasn't easy. I raised my head.

Guver smiled down at me. "Your exertions," he said, "were doubtless too much for you."

"You followed us," I said accusingly. My voice had all the punch of a wet flower bed.

"Of course," he said. "We *let* you escape. But you were under observation at all times."

"How?"

"Our resources in this area," he said, "are greater than appearances might lead you to expect." He grinned. "Once you had reached your destination, it was a simple matter for us to board a copter and join you."

"Us?"

Guver nodded, began backing up. I half turned, expecting to see a bunch of troopers, armed to the teeth. But I was wrong. A pair of electrolanterns glowed on the ground, showed Gem, the Supreme Potentate, standing back in the cave, the five other members of the High Council with him.

Two of 'em held lasers trained on us.

Laura sat up, took in our visitors. "The whole darn government's here," she said wonderingly.

"Sure," I said. "Don't you think we rate that kind of attention?"

Gem spoke, his voice echoing through the cave. "You rate nothing! For years there have been rumors of a secret weapon hidden away by this Jrb, one that could shake our society to its very roots."

"Its roots," I said, "are *you*."

"So they are," he said heartily. "That is why we could trust only ourselves to come here."

"But how did you know," I said, "that we would lead you to it?"

"We didn't," Gem said. "Irk knew."

Irk was Guver. He looked confused. "It was," he said, "it was a *feeling*."

Gem glared at us sternly. "Your usefulness is now over."

"I'm good at making repairs," I said. "I tell jokes. I have other talents, too."

"You will die," Gem said.

"Press the left key," the Crystal told me.

My hand was already resting on the base of the Destabilizer. I reached up, as though gripping the keyboard for support, and pressed the left key.

"Kill them," Gem said.

The two guys with the lasers pitched forward, fell flat on their faces. Gem shuddered, sank to his knees. The three other council members swayed like saplings in a tornado, keeled over to join their comrades in a heartening display of unity.

Only Guver somehow remained on his feet. He began

slowly, hesitantly, stepping toward us, like an infant who had just learned to walk.

The world was spinning before my eyes like a merry-go-round. I blinked, drew my laser. The assault on my senses wasn't as total this time. I could see well enough to shoot. It was them or us, and I was definitely partial to the us side—prejudiced in our favor, in fact. Guver made the best target. He would be the first to go.

"No!" the Crystal said.

"No? What kind of a thing is that to say?"

"He's one of us," the Crystal all but shouted, its voice sounding strong and confident now. "I am guiding him toward us. I understand, you see—"

A giant voice cut him short, filled the cave. "MY CHILDREN," it roared. The voice seemed to suspend all movement, hold everyone in thrall. All but Guver, who, step by step, drew closer. "I, THE VOICE OF TREX, GREET YOU," the voice boomed. "THERE IS CRYSTAL IN THIS CAVE, A RAW NATURAL FORMATION. BY ITSELF, IT IS DORMANT. BUT FOR MY VOICE TO HAVE BEEN ACTIVATED, OTHER PARTS OF CRYSTAL, THOSE FROM MAGALONE, MUST BE PRESENT IN THE CAVE. COMPLETION THEN IS AT HAND. I CONGRATULATE YOU. YOU WILL KNOW WHAT TO DO."

The voice cut out.

In the silence, Laura whispered, "What do we know to do?"

"You're asking me?"

"He means *me*," the Crystal said. "*I* know."

"Glad someone does."

Guver took three more steps, toppled over in my arms. "The Klarr," he croaked, "the Klarr—"

"What about 'em?" I could feel the power sweeping through me. Suddenly I was restored, all signs of weakness gone.

"They used me . . . . I didn't know—"

"Thomas!" Laura shrieked.

My head jerked up.

I wasn't the only one restored. Gem and his High Council were rising to their feet. Only it was a High Council straight from Hell. Their bodies were hunched and distorted, their faces resembled nothing so much as gigantic bee heads. I felt myself gagging, my well-advertised tolerance for all species slipping away.

"Take cover!" the Crystal yelled.

I took the hint, rolled behind the Destabilizer, dragging Guver with me. Laura was already huddled there.

Laser blasts singed the ground around us, the walls to our left and right.

I peered from behind Trex's creation, aiming my laser. The High Council was out of sight. Boulders hid them. Great.

The electrolanterns clicked off, by remote.

A white streak cut the darkness, almost singed my hairline.

"They want the Destabilizer," the Crystal said. "But they will destroy it in order to kill you."

"Us," I said. "Not 'you,' *us*."

"I quite understand," the Crystal said.

"They blocked my mind," Guver moaned. "I knew about Magalone, yet didn't. You see?"

"No."

"Use the weapon," the Crystal said.

"How?"

"Press the left key."

That was something I knew how to do; I'd had practice.
I pressed it.

The minicomputer lit up, the dials began to spin, the
lights to blink.

The Klarr got the message; their lasers began blasting
directly at the Destabilizer.

"Pull the lever," the Crystal said.

I pulled.

The cave blinked out.

And in that instant, we were back in Trex's lab on
Magalone.

Nothing had changed.

The director was up in his seat by the Destabilizer,
his fingers poised above the keyboard. XX41 and the
other mechs were racing toward him. The four walls that
were the lab computer were pulsing: lights blinking,
dials, vectors, and gauges spinning wildly, symbols
flashing on a dozen screens.

The protective seal was gone from over the lab, the
enemy missiles seconds way.

Trex pulled the lever.

The mechs froze. I froze. The whole lab held its breath.
A second crept by like an aging spider. Then another.

No missiles came plunging down. The Destabilizer
was still in one piece. Along with us.

"Whaddya know," I said weakly.

Trex's face broke into a huge grin. "Success!" he
chortled. "Success! Sweet, sweet, success!"

The guy had a point.

I let my breath out, wiped my brow with a shaky hand,
and turned to Laura.

She looked a bit limp, too. I reached out, took her

hand, and smiled. Both our hands shook in unison, a sure sign of true love.

"He said success," I said hoarsely. "Must mean we go on living, eh?"

"Ask him for lots more gold bricks, Thomas," she whispered. "We've earned them."

I shrugged. "He'll never believe me."

"Oh, yes he will," the Crystal said. "*I'll* tell him."

CHAPTER **31**

"Have another gold brick, Doc," I said.
       "Don't mind if I do," Dr. Sass said.
The gold bricks were piled on my desk. A bottle of
champagne and three goblets were keeping them company. Outside, through my windows, I could see a good
stretch of Happy City. It'd never looked so good.
Laura took a sip of champagne. "Go on," she said,
"finish the story."
"Yes, indeed," Sass said, moving another gold brick
to his pile. "By all means. It's quite fascinating."
"Only in the telling. Living it was strictly for the birds.
Anyway," I said, "when the Destabilizer and Ul missiles
collided that first time, the Klarr, hanging around too
close, were dragged along with the rest of us to the Great
Niche world."

209

"Because of the raw Crystal deposit there," Sass said, giving us a cherubic grin.

"Yeah, it acted like a magnet, pulled us all in. But we were scattered time-wise. Depending on where we'd been in relation to the Destabilizer, according to the Crystal. Guver and the Klarr turned up at the same time, in the same place. Not so hot for him."

"The Klarr blocked part of his memory," Laura said. "Part of him knew he was Guver, retained all of Guver's knowledge. But it didn't register. He thought of himself as Irk."

"They needed a front man," I said, "and Guver fit the bill perfectly. He looked like a native and was skilled in intrigue. Remember, the Klarr were trapped there, too. And there were only six of 'em."

"But they did not come empty-handed," Sass said, beaming the way a man does when he's come into sudden wealth.

"Uh uh. These guys were the vanguard of an invasion force, a sort of scouting party. They had plenty of superior hardware in tow, and the Destabilizer brought it all through. A hypno-beam let the Klarr assume the guise of natives, but they needed lots of privacy, according to Guver, because it was an intelligence device, only meant to work for short periods of time. That's why Guver was invaluable as a stooge."

"Even that change seemed natural to the poor man," Laura told Sass. "That's how much the hypno-beam had him under its thumb."

"Plf the Third was no match for the Klarr weapons," I said. "He fell. His world was already a centralized dictatorship. The Klarr just took it a step further, segmented it along Ul lines. Guver gave 'em the inside track.

Made control that much easier.''

"The hypno-beam suppressed the Crystal in Guver,'' Laura said, "which was why our Crystal didn't spot it.''

"And in the Klarr, my dear?'' Sass said, reaching for his goblet. "Surely it was there, too?''

"It was there, all right,'' she said. "But inactive. The Klarr were just too alien for the Crystal to function the way it did in us.''

"In the cave,'' I said, "the raw Crystal, acting on ours, knocked us all for a loop. Even the Klarr, shorting the hypno-beam and stripping 'em of their cover.''

"The raw Crystal was the power source,'' Laura said. "But it was dormant. It needed a heavy douse of Magalone Crystal to spark it. Thomas and I alone might not have been enough, but we, Guver, and the six Klarr, were just right. The left key Thomas punched completed the circuit between both Crystals. And the Destabilizer came alive.''

"Whipped us right back to Magalone,'' I said. "Like electricity shot through a wire.''

"The Crystal,'' Laura said, "became a mountain again—''

"Yeah,'' I broke in, "instead of our lifetime companion. Thank god.''

"And,'' Laura continued, "absorbed most of the blast this time.''

"The 'wire,' '' I said, "was still strung between both worlds. The cave Crystal siphoned off the overload.''

"And the war with the Ul?'' Sass asked.

"Over,'' I said. "The vile Ul and Magalone have buried the hatchet, at least for now, and united against the even viler Klarr.''

"Ah, the Crystal convinced Dr. Trex then?''

"The Klarr convinced him. They'd come along for the ride, but nobody noticed in the excitement. They turned up on our monitors trying to skip the building, and our mechs nabbed 'em.''

"So what happens to Guver now?" Laura asked.

"Nothing," I said. "As his world's greatest living expert on the Klarr, he'll probably get a promotion. Guy's middle-aged again. Should go a long way, maybe even become dictator someday.''

"That's *director*," Laura said.

"Not with Guver running the works, sweetie.''

"And our poor mechs?" she said.

"Seemed fine the last time I looked.''

"I mean," she said, "the ones who died on that awful world.''

"Those, eh? Well, we've just got the dumb paper's word that they died. Plf's press wasn't worth much. Our mechs might've holed up somewhere, they're good for the long haul. For all we know, honey, they may be leading the revolution on the Great Niche right now.''

"*What* revolution?"

"Well, with the Klarr gone, and some of our hardware in native hands, there's bound to be a revolution. It's only a matter of time.''

Sass beamed. "A splendid job. And profitable, too." He drained his goblet. "I have good news for you.''

"Good news?" I said. "For *me*?"

"What would you say, Dunjer, if I told you I had an even better job for you?"

Laura and I exchanged glances.

I emptied my goblet in a single gulp, set it down on the desk. My hand wasn't even shaking. "Death first," I said with simple dignity.

PRESENTING THE ADVENTURES OF

BY HARRY HARRISON

BILL, THE GALACTIC HERO

00395-3/$3.95 US/$4.95 Can

He was just an ordinary guy named Bill, a fertilizer operator from a planet of farmers. Then a recruiting robot shanghaied him with knockout drops, and he came to in deep space, aboard the Empire warship *Christine Keeler*.

BILL, THE GALACTIC HERO: THE PLANET OF ROBOT SLAVES   75661-7/$3.95 US/$4.95 Can

BILL, THE GALACTIC HERO: ON THE PLANET OF BOTTLED BRAINS   75662-5/$3.95 US/$4.95 Can
(co-authored by Robert Sheckley)

BILL, THE GALACTIC HERO: ON THE PLANET OF TASTELESS PLEASURE   75664-1/$3.95 US/$4.95 Can
(co-authored by David Bischoff)

BILL, THE GALACTIC HERO: ON THE PLANET OF ZOMBIE VAMPIRES   75665-X/$3.95 US/$4.95 Can
(co-authored by Jack C. Haldeman II)

BILL, THE GALACTIC HERO: ON THE PLANET OF TEN THOUSAND BARS   75666-8/$3.99 US/$4.99 Can
(co-authored by David Bischoff)

THE CONTINUATION
OF THE FABULOUS
INCARNATIONS OF IMMORTALITY
SERIES

PIERS ANTHONY

FOR LOVE OF EVIL
75285-9/$4.95 US/$5.95 Can

AND ETERNITY
75286-7/$4.95 US/$5.95 Can

ARTHUR C. CLARKE'S VENUS PRIME

by Paul Preuss

VOLUME 6: THE SHINING ONES 75350-2/$3.95 US/$4.95 CAN
The ever capable Sparta proves the downfall of the mysterious and sinister organization that has been trying to manipulate human history.

VOLUME 5: THE DIAMOND MOON

75349-9/$3.95 US/$4.95 CAN
Sparta's mission is to monitor the exploration of Jupiter's moon, Amalthea, by the renowned Professor J.Q.R. Forester.

VOLUME 4: THE MEDUSA ENCOUNTER

75348-0/$3.95 US/$4.95 CAN
Sparta's recovery from her last mission is interrupted as she sets out on an interplanetary investigation of her host, the Space Board.

VOLUME 3: HIDE AND SEEK 75346-4/$3.95 US/$4.95 CAN

VOLUME 2: MAELSTROM 75345-6/$3.95 US/$4.95 CAN

VOLUME 1: BREAKING STRAIN 75344-8/$3.95 US/$4.95 CAN

Each volume features a special technical infopak,
including blueprints of the structures of *Venus Prime*